The Rebel C

Copyright © 2021 A. Bean
Cover illustrated/designed by Valicity Elaine

All rights reserved. No part of this publication may be reproduced, distributed, or transmitted in any form or by any means, including photocopying, recording, or other electronic or mechanical methods, without the prior written permission of the publisher, except in the case of brief quotations embodied in critical reviews and certain other noncommercial uses permitted by copyright law. For permission requests, write to the publisher, addressed "Attention: Permissions Coordinator," at the address below.

ISBN: 9781957290041 (eBook)
ISBN: 9781957290058 (print)

This is a work of fiction. Any references to historical events, real people, or real places are used fictitiously. Names, characters, and places are products of the author's imagination. Inclusion of or reference to any Christian elements or themes are used in a fictitious manner and are not meant to be perceived or interpreted as an act of disrespect against such a wonderful and beautiful belief system.

The Rebel Christian Publishing
350 Northern Blvd STE 324 – 1390
Albany, NY 12204

Visit us: http://www.therebelchristian.com/
Email us: rebel@therebelchristian.com

Contents

Chapter One 1

Chapter Two 23

Chapter Three 45

Chapter Four 67

Chapter Five 82

Chapter Six 92

Chapter Seven 105

Chapter Eight 123

Chapter Nine 140

Chapter Ten 152

Chapter Eleven 164

Chapter Twelve 176

Chapter Thirteen 192

Chapter Fourteen 208

Chapter Fifteen 220

ACKNOWLEDGEMENTS 239

The Rebel Christian Publishing 240

Original Author's Notes 241

This novel was originally published as an episodic story on the Kindle Vella platform. It has been modified and formatted for your enjoyment. Original author's notes can be found at the very end of the book. Please enjoy **The Scribe** and take the time to leave your thoughts and opinion in a review on Amazon, Bookbub, and Goodreads. Thank you!

Other Books by A. Bean

Too Young

The End of the World series

The End of the World
The New World Order
Book III (Coming April 2022)

For you... You are so very special to me, thank you for being with me on this journey, old friend.

The Scribe

A. Bean

A Rebel Christian Publishing Book

Chapter One
The Merchant Girl

"Ma, I'm leaving now!"

"Ok, darling. I'll bring your shawl." Ma emerged from the dark hallway, holding a ragged shawl in her gnarled hands. She gripped it tightly, fingers bent at the knuckles as if still holding her ever-present sewing needle. Mother was an expert seamstress, she had to be, because we sold her scarves and things at the market for fair coin. We weren't hungry, but we needed every copper we earned. Thankfully, winter would be here soon, so Ma was swimming in requests.

"I don't need my shawl anymore," I said, pushing it away.

She frowned. "Why not?"

"I'm old enough to work, which means I don't have to cover up anymore." She regarded me in silence, taking in my bare shoulders and slender legs in one aversive tick. Keeping my eyes on the floor, I mumbled one last, pitiful argument. "It's not even cold yet."

She harrumphed. "I know you're sixteen now, but you're still my baby." Ma kissed my forehead as she wrapped the shawl around my shoulders. "And it *is* very cold out there."

I pulled away. "Do you think Father is getting better?"

"Not better—but not any worse, either; so that's a good sign."

I chewed my lip, mentally rearranging my schedule for the day. If I finished early at the market, I could run up the road and see if Mr. Hemmindale needed a hand. Sometimes the old farmer would offer coin for help. Just a few hours up there and I'd be back by dinner.

Ma poked me in the chest. "Don't worry about your father. I know you've been selling goods for Mr. Hemmindale, and I'm proud of you for that, but we have enough to make it through winter."

"Mama—"

"That means I want you home early today." She crossed her arms, thick arms with dark brown skin stretched over them. Mama was what they called a "big country woman." Heavy in the hips, strong legs, and thick shoulders with meaty arms, like she could punch you to death.

I took a breath. "I'll try, Mama. But what if it snows too much and I can't get to the market, or what if you get too tired to sew? Let me work a little more." She looked about ready to ball up those big fists of hers, so I grabbed her hands and held them in mine. "If I work more, you can take some time off or at least spend Christmas Day without a needle in your hand."

She nodded. "Fine, but at least be home for dinner. I hate eating alone every night."

"Yes!" I squealed. I hugged her tightly and swung my satchel over my shoulder. "I'll see you at dinner!"

"You be careful out there in the market, Amana." She was walking behind me, flat feet taking steps so big she nearly scratched my heals with her toes.

"I know, Ma. Be careful and be home by dinner."

She sighed. "The market is no place for a young girl. You shouldn't be *working*; my baby should be getting ready for marriage."

"Why would I marry right now? I'm at the peak of my career." *Peak* was a stretch; Ma was overworked, Dad was sick, and I was hustling so hard my bunions had bunions. But, for a poor girl from the sticks, I wasn't doing *so* bad.

Mama grabbed my shoulders and turned me around. "What career is that, young lady?"

"You already know I'm gonna be a Scribe."

"Absolutely not."

"But, Mama—"

"Favian Amana Hart!" She crossed her arms, rolling her neck like she was ready to fight me. "That is the end of this conversation. Now hurry along before you lose your spot at the market."

I wanted to argue more but I wasn't stupid. I kissed her on the cheek and turned to leave. "Bye, Mama."

"Back by dinner!" She was yelling from the porch now, her voice louder than the stirring wind.

I rolled my eyes as I pulled the ragged shawl tighter around me. She was right, it was cold out.

On my donkey, I rode down to the market with my cart full of Ma's things; blankets, bags, scarves, and shirts. The dirt roads were still damp from the morning rain which made it tough for Ruby to trudge along. Eventually, I hopped off and walked beside her. I didn't mind the stroll, walking kept me warm.

When we finally arrived, I tied Ruby to her usual post and started setting up.

"Good morning, Amana. How's your father?" a voice asked over my shoulder.

"Morning, Mr. Castillo, he's hanging in there. To be honest, I'm more worried about the weather. We had frost this morning."

"That means winter is gonna be harsh. You guys sure you'll be fine?"

I shrugged a bony shoulder. "I'm working extra."

"Smart girl." He nodded, rubbing his leathery chin. "You know I'm only two shacks down, just come on over and my family will help if you need it."

I didn't want his help, but I also didn't want to be rude, so I said, "Thanks," and turned away.

Mr. Castillo went on. "You should be enjoying your life, Amana, not working all day. But don't worry, God's looking out for you."

"He sure is," I agreed, hammering a peg for my tent. "I'll come by soon as I can, how's that sound?"

"That sounds perfect."

I waved to the older man and he tipped his hat at me. As I started on the next peg, I heard a voice cackling behind me.

"Why do they let hags into the market?"

I kept hammering, happy to hit something.

"I'm talking to you!" the voice shouted. When I didn't turn around, he kept on picking fun. "You'll never find a proper husband working out here. You'll always be a hag."

"Well, let me be a hag in peace, then." He stopped his cackling, but I still didn't face him; I just gripped my hammer tighter as I heard him move closer.

He crouched behind me, his rank breath rolling up my

neck as he said, "Since no one's gonna have you, at least I will."

I clutched my hammer as he leaned forward but everything stopped when Mrs. Castillo yelled, "Henry, you better leave that girl alone or else I'm telling your mother!"

Henry huffed but straightened up without a word. His family sold fish here in the market, they needed to be here as badly as I did, so if he got caught acting out, they'd probably get banned from doing business. This wasn't his first time picking on me, but I hoped it would be his last.

"You alright?" Mrs. Castillo asked. She marched over and offered a bowl of water which I guzzled so fast I nearly choked. She leaned in real close, so no one else could hear. "If something like that happens again, you tell my husband."

I wiped the sweat from my forehead. "I was scared."

"I know." She hugged me tight. "Just let me know if you need anything. I'll send my boy, Ray, over to help."

"Thanks, Mrs. Castillo, but I'm sure I'll be fine."

"It's no bother." She shook her head, thick lips spreading in a wide smile. "Ray loves helping out. Especially since my husband is good friends with your father."

I nodded, trying not to think of my dad. My face must have given me away because Mrs. Castillo touched my arm and said, "I should go now, sweetie." Then she turned and went back to her tent, her honey toned skin glowing in the sunlight.

With my tent up and the market open, I got busy shouting sales to the folk walking through. Ma's stuff was good, but I wasn't getting many biters, so after an hour I took a break just to rest my voice. As if on cue, Ray ambled over when I was petting Ruby, wearing a shy smile and giving me a little wave.

He fed her a carrot stick and said, "Sorry I didn't come over earlier."

"Don't worry about it."

"Is your mother making new products for the winter already?"

I nodded, watching him stare at her fabric. "We're starting early since Ma thinks winter will be bad this year."

Ray rubbed his tan hand along the pale woolen quilt. I watched his dark eyes rove over my mother's work. He seemed intrigued when he said, "Your mom's gonna make a fortune with this. Look at those details in the stitching. She gets better and better."

"She does," I said plainly. Heavy brows furrowed at me which made me nervous. "What?"

"You're worried about her, aren't you?"

"I'm worried about everything, Ray." I did not want to have this conversation right now, but he kept going. "It's not like you to avoid praising your mother's work. I remember the first day we met, you were so adamant about the quality of her work, you wouldn't let anyone buy it for less than a dozen pisces." We both laughed at the same time, and all at once I remembered why he was my best friend. Ray, with his long legs and lanky arms, his shy smile and gentle stubbornness. He always made me forget all the bad parts of my life.

"You're right," I exhaled. "I'm really worried about Ma. It's been a year and eight months since my dad got sick. She's working every day, exhausting herself. I help out where I can, but I don't know the craft the way she does. I'm only good for selling."

"Well," Ray looked around nervously and then moved closer. "Are you still trying to become a Scribe?"

"Of course. But I've got no clue how."

He leaned away, eyebrow raised, doubt disfiguring his otherwise handsome face. "I thought Scribes were called from birth. Magically knew how to do all the reading and writing and speaking languages."

I crossed my arms. "What are you saying?"

"If you were really meant to be a Scribe, you'd know how to become one."

"Maybe I'll figure it out later. Or maybe that part of the legend is just a myth." He gave me the side eye, which made me want to hit him. "C'mon, Ray, you *know* I'm meant to be a Scribe."

"*Or* you're meant to be a normal girl." He grinned.

"Whose sixteen now. And should be getting married. Right?"

"Shouldn't *you* be getting married?" I countered. "You're a little old to be single, even for a boy. Two more years and you'll be a drunkard known in every brothel."

"Shut up," Ray grumbled. "I've been waiting for someone, that's all."

"Do I know her?"

He smiled a big, goofy smile that made me grin back. I always liked when Ray was happy like this. He was handsome with a smile on his face, and even though he was getting older, age had been kind to him. Women crowded his parents' tent whenever he was there; they were glancing at us now, undoubtedly wondering what we were talking about.

"I'm sure you know her," he said. "She's a bit lost right now, though. When she comes back, I'll introduce you guys." He waved a hand and left my tent for his, but I didn't get to watch him go because a cheery voice shouted beside me, "Morning, Amana!"

"Morning, Mr. Tosh." I turned to greet him. "How can I help you today?"

"I'd like to place an order. I hear there's been frost in some parts."

"There has," I nodded. "Are you trying to beat the winter rush?"

"Of course! How far out is your mother booked?"

"Until winter's *normal* first frost."

He rubbed his chin. "Can you get me in that six-week window if I pay a little extra for a rush order?"

I smiled and snuck a glance over at Ray. He was entertaining a customer, but he finally looked up and noticed me when she stepped away. A smile instantly split his face. It was Ray who taught me how to hustle better than anyone.

I leaned closer to Mr. Tosh, just like Ray taught me, and asked, "How much extra are you talking?" Smiling makes the whole thing seem like a negotiation, so I grinned real big. But I already had a price in my head; Mr. Tosh was falling right into my favorite game.

"Well, I can offer you three extra pisces and a copper piece."

I raised an eyebrow. "It's been a while since I've gone home with a copper piece. I'm kinda hoping to stay away from those copper days."

"Well, maybe not a copper piece. Maybe five extra pisces."

"Five extra is only worth a small quilt." I blew a heavy sigh, like I was disappointed in him. "I'm gonna need more than that if you really want to get that six-week timeframe."

Mr. Tosh swallowed, staring at the fabric longingly. He

looked like he was ready to change his mind, so I added, "That frost will be snow pretty soon. Better make a decision quick."

His shoulders slumped and I knew I'd won. Mr. Tosh shook his head, his pudgy chin wobbled with the motion, and straightened his back. He looked confident, for the first time ever. "I can offer you one extra silver callios."

I smiled. "Now we're talking."

Mr. Tosh pulled out his coin purse. I could practically smell the gold and silver and copper coins all mixed up in there, waiting for me to claim them.

"Let me make an even better offer," I said, leaning close again. "One silver callios and two pisces and you'll be in the *three*-week window."

Sweat broke out on his pale nose. "Three-week window?"

"Now, now," I help up my hands to calm him down. "Winter could hit at any moment, so that's not a guarantee—but it does mean you'll get your order before anyone else once the weather settles."

Ray had taught me a lot, but I taught him how to gauge. He'd always said you could tell who'd give in to your offers, but he didn't know there was extra money to be made. Having Mr. Tosh pay the extra two pisces wasn't just extra money, it was payment on two more items at my shop. That way, I'd be making double profit off those items.

Mr. Tosh thought a hard moment, his chin quivering in anxiety. "Just two more pisces?"

"Just two."

He extended his hand. "Deal."

"Perfect!" I said, shaking his sweaty palm. "Today you'll owe the extra pisces and pay the rest on pickup."

"You need the extra today?"

"This is time sensitive; I need to show something to Ma to make this rush order worth it."

He nodded, probably thinking about Ma's meaty arms and wild temper. "I guess you're right." He dug into his purse and passed me two square coins.

"Thank you, Mr. Tosh. Now, what's the order?"

As Mr. Tosh rambled off his order, I jotted it down using words and numbers known to all the common folk. He left with a nervous smile and another handshake, leaving room for more customers to pile into the small tent. I worked hard to keep all the orders straight, but when it became overwhelming, Ray came by and helped out for a bit until his parents needed him back. I loved every second he helped; Ray was good at getting the lady clients to agree to unbelievable prices. With him stopping in, I could nearly double my weekly profit. He never asked for any money in return and always turned down my offer to pay for his help. Instead, he liked to drag me down to the farm to grab peaches and vegetables to sell. Every now and then, he'd let me buy him a bushel of corn.

As the market closed and I began to take down my tent, I heard Ray call over to me, "Are you going to the farm later?"

"I told Ma I'd be home by dinner, but ... if you're going, I'm going."

He snorted and turned back to his tent. "I've gotta help my dad pack up first, so don't leave without me."

As I waited on my donkey for Murray—he hated his real name—I thought about what it would be like to really be a Scribe. To be rich, to have the best medicine, and to live a good life, not a hard one like mine. Deep down, it wasn't the money I really wanted. It was the *knowledge*— the ability to understand every spoken language, to read books so old the pages crumbled in your fingers. Hardly anyone around here could read, that was a gift you had to be born with. If you were fortunate, you could *learn* to read, but that took decades. In a world with harsh winters and scorching summers, you needed to spend all your time in the field. Not reading crumbly books. Still ... I longed for more as I sat on Ruby, watching bent backs and tired faces hobble by.

"You ready?" Ray asked, jogging over.

"Ready," I said.

We took off on our donkeys. Normally, Ray and I

would chat a lot, but today he seemed deep in thought. I watched his figure in the sleeping sunlight as we rode along the bumpy road. He looked tired, but it seemed his thoughts were keeping him from falling asleep. I remember the first time we rode home together. He'd offered to ride with me to make sure I made it home safe. We had already known each other for a few months by then, and he'd never offered before. I still don't understand what made him offer that day, but I'm glad he did because our ride together forged the bond we have now. That day, he found out about my ability to understand different languages.

When I close my eyes, I can perfectly recall every detail of that day. How he'd asked me about my sales and offered to help pack up my tent. The way he looked when he dipped his head and smiled shyly. What I remember most vividly is the moment he ran back to his tent to tell his mother he'd be riding home with me. They spoke in hushed voices, with him bent over to hear his mother more clearly. Then, when he straightened to leave, he kissed her cheek and said, "*Te amo, Mama*."

I'd been staring at him so long, he looked at me funny when he jogged back over. "Are you ready?"

"Y—yes!" I stuttered dumbly. "I was just thinking how sweet it is that you tell your mother you love her before you leave."

I giggled, thinking I should probably say that to my

mother more often, but Ray wasn't laughing. He was just staring at me, wide-eyed and open-mouthed, like I'd just insulted him somehow.

He said, "*Hablas*," and just stared at me some more.

It got real awkward with us just looking at each other, so I hopped on Ruby and he hopped on his donkey and we rode in silence for a few minutes. Then he said it again.

"*Hablas*…"

"Speak what?" I said. "Spanish? No, I don't speak it. I just understand it." I tapped my chin, thinking for a quick second. "Actually, I *can* speak Spanish. I just never had to."

Ray pulled his donkey to a complete stop.

"What's wrong?" I stopped, too.

"Who taught you Spanish?"

"No one? I just know how to speak it."

"So you just *know* Spanish? No teaching, no nothin'?" He was looking real serious now, his brow all furrowed and his full lips pressed into a hard line. I'd never seen him that way before, so I said, "Si, hablo espanol y otras idiomas. Por que?"

"Por que? Porque solo escribas conocen diferentes idiomas. Y todos los escribas son hombres ricos no mujeres!" he yelled.

I exhaled and said, "I know."

"You know?"

"*Yes*," I repeated, getting angry. "I know multiple

languages. And I also know that only Scribes have this ability—and I know Scribes are only rich men." I crossed my arms and mumbled, "Not women."

Ray looked away, stunned.

"This is why I never talk about it." Not just because it freaked people out, but because it was a gift only Scribes could have. Reading and speaking other languages wasn't something you learned; when you were a Scribe, you were born already knowing those things. Somehow, I knew how to read before I'd ever seen a book. I understood Spanish perfectly even though I'd never heard the language before that moment. Knowledge wasn't something to gain as a Scribe, it was something you owned.

There were people like Ray, too. Ones who weren't born already knowing things but had the ability to learn. That's how come he was bilingual, and his parents were, too. But most people were like dumb Henry; not knowing a thing other than the common language and never being able to learn how to read or write it. They weren't illiterate because they were *stupid*; they just couldn't comprehend written words and letters. It was like they were born with blinders on.

"Then why did you talk about it with me?" Ray was asking.

I snapped my head toward him so I could give him my meanest glare. "It was an accident."

"I won't tell anyone," he said softly.

We started riding again, and after a few moments of silence, Ray said, "How did you discover it?"

"That I'm a Scribe?"

He flinched and looked around nervously. "Don't talk so loud. There've been women in the past who claimed to have scribal abilities—"

"I know that."

"Do you know they were seen as witches who mocked God? And that they were all burned alive?"

"Yes, I do! But do *you* know how many women *weren't* lying and actually died senselessly? It's sad. But I've gotta do something."

"What can you do?"

I gripped the reins on my donkey, squeezing so hard my hands began to shake. "I don't know yet. But I do know I'm meant to be a Scribe. I found out when I was ten years old, and my dad was dealing with some customers. He asked me to jot down the orders while he took care of something else. After the customers left, he looked at the notes I'd written and realized they weren't in the common language."

"What language were they in?" Ray asked.

I chewed my lip, unsure if I should tell him. But I'd already said this much. "French," I confessed. "I don't even know why I wrote them down in French. It just kinda happened. And ever since then, I've been trying to figure out a way to get into the Scribal School. They say some women with good reading and good handwriting at least make it into the teaching subdivision. So maybe I'll go for that."

Ray pursed his lips. "The Scribal school costs a lot of coin. You have to be rich for that to happen."

"I know that."

Ruby hit a bump, jolting me from my daydreams. We'd made it to the farm, faster than I expected. I stretched and glanced at Ray, he was still tense and frowning.

"You alright? We didn't talk at all during the ride."

"I'm fine. I just got caught up in my thoughts, you know?"

I smirked.

"What?"

"You thinkin' about that girl, I bet."

He smirked back. "Actually, I was."

I wasn't expecting that answer, so I shut my mouth and hopped off my donkey. Mr. Hemmindale was waiting by the barn in his dirty boots and overalls. I waved at him and forced a smile, which he noticed right away.

"You guys fighting or something?"

"No. Ray's just being Ray and I don't wanna pry."

He chuckled, then coughed up some phlegm and spat it

into the grass. "You know Ray is a man now, Amana. He's got a lot to think about, inching on past the age of wedding in two years and all. He's still trying to make a name for himself so some lucky lady will want to snatch him up."

"Yep," I grunted, straightening the headscarf wrapped around my hair. "Ray is a man now, I know that. But I'm a woman now, too."

"That's very true." Mr. Hemmindale blinked and then his face changed. "It don't look good, now that I think about it."

"What don't look good?" I asked.

"An unmarried man and woman hanging out. Going places together…" he trailed off and it finally hit me.

I squinted. "Ray and I are just friends. He's got someone he's thinking of already. And I just turned sixteen—Ray is eighteen now, he'll be too old for me soon." I chuckled but Mr. Hemmindale did not. "Am I missing something?" I asked.

He looked over at Ray and sighed. "I'm sure you are. But, look, I've got a big order here. It's gonna be a day's journey, so I'll be paying you for your travel as well."

I ignored his last statement. "What am I missing?"

"Sometimes us old farts just talk nonsense," he insisted. "Now come on, so you can get this order correct. Ray, can you cover for Amana at the market tomorrow?"

"He doesn't have to; Ma will go if I can't. Dad sleeps

most of the day so it's alright if he's alone for a few hours."

"I can cover for her," Ray said, jogging over.

I gave him a smile and mouthed the words, '*I owe you.*'

"This order is huge," Mr. Hemmindale explained, guiding me into the barn. "You'll have to use my cart. I'll give you my merchant's pass to get in and out of the city. Look for a man named Ben Jones. He'll take the cart from you and hook it up to his horse. Once he gives you the money, you're free to go home."

"How much am I expecting from this Ben guy? Must be pretty rich to have a horse."

"He works for a rich guy. And they're paying some clean copper for this cart, so I'm gonna treat you real good with this one. It means a lot that you're taking a full day off from work just to go up there for my farm."

"You always pay me well, Mr. Hemmindale," I said. "It's no problem."

He nodded, then hacked up more phlegm. "Meet me here in front of the barn tomorrow morning. I'll have everything ready for you."

"I'll see you tomorrow morning," I said. "Just before sunrise."

* * *

As Ray and I rode back, I was stuck in my head, trying to

find the right words to start a conversation. Ray beat me to it.

"I'm sorry. This whole time I've been thinkin' and not paying any attention."

"Don't apologize," I said, waving my hand.

He gave me a sideways glance. "I've just been thinking of this girl a lot now. But I don't really know if she thinks of me."

Not this again. "So, this girl made you totally shut down?"

"Well," he rubbed the back of his neck. "My parents were also giving me a hard time towards the end of the day."

"What happened?"

"There was a girl there, a wealthy girl—"

"She couldn't be that wealthy if she was buying stuff herself."

Ray snorted and I couldn't help but smile, happy to see him back to normal again. At least a *little* normal.

"I said the same thing. But that doesn't really matter to my folks. They're obsessed with finding me a wife because I'm old."

"Ma is obsessed with finding me a husband because I'm young."

He chuckled. "I don't want to marry someone just because I'm running out of time or because someone looks wealthy. I know I don't have much, but I'm still a good man. I think it's worth the wait if it means finding the right woman." His sigh was weighed down with sorrow.

"It's your heart, Ray. You do with it what you will," I said.

Ray suddenly looked relieved. "What do you know about romance?" he joked. "The only thing you love is selling at the market."

I tossed my head back and laughed loudly. "You'll never believe what I got out of Mr. Tosh today."

And just like that, Ray and I were back to our normal selves again.

Chapter Two
The Rich and The Poor

The next morning, I left my cart for Ray and his family to take to the market while I was gone. I told Ray he could keep a portion of the earnings for helping out, but he said his mother preferred blankets and baby clothes for his sister, Lolita. She isn't here yet, but Mrs. Castillo is due sometime this winter, so the clothes were a good exchange.

With all that business out the way, I finally took off. A few hours with Ruby went by faster than I thought. Ruby was good company; she listened when I spoke, and I swear she grunted a reply when I was done. We talked about all kinds of things; Ray and his family, Ma and her sewing, even this job I'm thankful for. I talked so much; I'm sure

Ruby was relieved when we finally arrived at the new town.

Thanks to the merchant's pass from Mr. Hemmindale, I didn't have to wait too long to get through the gates. As I rode through this strange town, I could tell it was a place only wealthy folk could live. Mr. Hemmindale had told me to dress my best for this delivery when I showed up at his barn this morning. I had to run back home and change, grumbling the whole time, but I was glad I listened as Ruby trudged on. There were no beggars or barefoot children on the road, no trash piled on the sidewalk, and no feces running through the streets. The air seemed cleaner, the sky brighter, even the women looked prettier than any ladies I'd ever seen.

I could feel my eyes bulging as I gawked at everything around me. Buildings that scraped the sky, horse and buggies trotting down the road, people draped in fancy clothes made from fabrics I couldn't name. Ma would have a heart attack seeing all this—I thought I was having one myself. I wanted to take in every little detail so I could tell Ray. The two of us would always fantasize about getting away from home and living in a place like this. If I ever become a Scribe, I could make our fantasies a reality. For now, I had to focus on finding Mr. Ben Jones.

I took Ruby around a corner and found a tree for us to hide in the shade. More faces passed us by, pretty and plump and glowing in the sun. But it was the face of a tall, slender man with dark hair that caught my eye. He pulled his horse up to me and hopped down without a problem, considering those long legs of his. His skinny fingers played with the golden chain of a pocket watch and his lips curved into a menacing grin.

I gave him a tight smile and glanced away, unsure if he was Mr. Jones. Beside us stood a building made of stacks of black bricks. There were windows all over it with studious people sitting behind them; they sat at desks and appeared to be a class of some sort. My eyes drifted to the sign atop the building, the words were written in formal English. It said, **The School of Knowledge**. I'd never seen anything like it. Before I knew it, I'd taken a step toward the structure, but the man called out to me.

"Excuse me! You're not allowed to be here."

I'd almost forgotten about the mysterious man in front of me. I took a step back and faced him. "Are you Mr. Ben Jones?"

"Who's asking?"

"I am."

He clicked his tongue. "You have no manners. Who are you to ask about me?"

"So you *are* Mr. Ben Jones." I crossed my arms.

"Who do you think you are, *peasant?*" He spat that word so hard I felt my knees buckle. I took a breath and thought of Mr. Hemmindale and Ray and Ma. I needed to finish this job more than I needed to start a pointless argument with a man I didn't even know.

"Sorry, Mr. Ben Jones," I said. "Mr. Hemmindale sent me here to deliver this cart and I got caught up staring at that beautiful building. I mean you no harm or disrespect."

He shifted his weight from one foot to the other and played with his pocket watch. "I see. You should have said so at first. And you should learn your place when you're talking to someone like me. I'm a Scribe, you know."

I gasped. "You are?"

"You didn't know?"

"No, I'm not from here. I'm from Blakenberge. I don't think my town has any Scribes."

"Of course not," he laughed. "Scribes don't come from poor towns. Can anything good come from Blakenberge? Absolutely not!" He wiped at his eyes, laughing so hard at his own joke. I was too excited about meeting a Scribe in person to even care about his manners. "Well now, peasant," he said, straightening his doublet, "I guess I better unload the cart myself. I don't know why Hemmindale would send a girl for this job."

"I was the only help available."

"You don't have a brother or a father?"

"I have a father, but he's very sick."

Ben raised an eyebrow, taking off his baldric and

carelessly tossing it over his horse's saddle. The dagger attached glinted in the sunlight as it swayed with the movement. I watched in amazement, wondering just how much his clothes cost and how talented his seamstress must be. Ben moved to unlatch the cart from Ruby. "So, it's just you? You came all the way here alone?"

"Yes."

"Hmph. Pretty dangerous for a woman to travel alone. I guess in your—"

"Excuse me," I interrupted him, I couldn't wait any longer to ask. "What is that building?" I didn't want him to know I could read or understand formal English, so I pretended not to know.

"Peasants truly have no manners," he mumbled to himself. "That building is a school for those fortunate enough to have been born with the Gift."

"The *Gift*," I repeated, giving him my best stupid face.

He went on, happy to educate this poor peasant girl. "Yes, the Gift. As in, the ability to learn. We Scribes do much of our training in that school."

I gaped at him. "What kind of training?"

"We tediously study every book we acquire. Dissecting it to make sure its story aligns with the history we've created."

Now I didn't have to act confused. I really had no idea what he was saying. "I don't understand," I said.

"Of course, you don't. But since you've been such a good little peasant, delivering this cart all by your lonesome, I'll explain it as best I can." Ben leaned against the cart, brushed his hair from his face. Ready to talk like we were friends. "Scribes are responsible for recording history—no—for *writing* history. Sometimes we simply refurbish old books in need of repair, but there are also times we find books in such poor condition that pages are missing, and entire sections are destroyed. That's when our true calling comes in. We rewrite the stories ourselves; filling in the blanks and molding the tale to what we need it to be."

I squinted. "So you pretend to be the book writer yourself?"

"The *author*," he corrected. "And yes. Every book ever written in the history of our world, has come from a Scribe—there have been some cases where those with the Gift chose their own paths. But we have made it our business to find and collect every book we can, to revise and release as necessary."

"That ain't right."

"And why not?" he harrumphed. "How would a girl like you even know? Only a tiny percentage of the population has the ability to learn to read—and only a portion of them ever *use* that ability. No one but us would know the true stories from the fakes."

"It's wrong because you're changing other people's work—stories they worked hard on themselves."

"Sometimes circumstance doesn't allow us to keep the original. We have the book's best interest in our hearts."

I crossed my arms. "And what about books that aren't made up stories? Things like memoires and biographies?"

He scoffed. "Scribes have the power to rewrite this world's history and mold humanity's future. Sometimes that means creating people, places, and even events throughout history."

My heart clenched in my chest. I wanted to scream. All my life I thought reading and writing was just things to do for fun. I had no idea what it truly was—what it could become. I'd heard my mama say it before, but it wasn't until that moment that I really understood. Knowledge is power. And some people could abuse that power. In a hundred years those uppity Scribes could decide my poor town never existed. Hundreds of generations would be blotted out of history with the stroke of a pen.

I didn't want to be a Scribe anymore, I *had* to be. If we were writing history and molding the future, I could make sure it would be done the right way. No more creating fake people to influence the course of history. No more erasing things the Scribes don't agree with. I could change everything. But first I had to enroll in the School of Knowledge.

"So," I said, digging my toes into the soft gras. I tried to sound as nonchalant as possible. "How do you get into the school?"

Ben went back to hooking up the cart. "We take in potential students when they're children, usually around age five. The testing period lasts until age eight; if the child isn't able to produce any evidence of the Gift during that timeframe, then they're sent away."

"And if they do show signs of having the learning Gift?"

"Then they're enrolled in scribal training. Most students move into the scribal house to stay focused. It's just between those woods—designed by trainees who specialize in architectural knowledge." He let go of a dreamy sigh. "It is really a work of art, if you ever get to see it."

I swallowed thickly. "Do women get to learn at the school?"

Ben was busy messing with the cart, but he stopped what he was doing when he heard my question. Turned around real slow, his dark eyes cutting me down like they were a sharp pair of knives. He watched me for a second too long, making my skin crawl as he twiddled his fingers, itching to play with the pocket watch tucked into his breast pocket. Then he finally unscrewed his jaw and said, "Young girls are allowed to get tested. But you must be able to afford the test—all three years of it. Which means it's not for peasants like yourself."

I lifted my chin, ready to argue, but he cut me off before the words could even leave my mouth. "You're too old. The school doesn't offer testing after age eight; by then, the mind has developed too much to learn the basics."

My shoulders slumped in defeat. I'd been trying all my life to find a way to become a Scribe, only to learn I was eight years too late. I wanted to cry but I held back the tears, straightened my shoulders, and marched over to help Ben with the cart. The faster he finished, the faster I could go home and talk it out with Ray. I needed his stubborn optimism right about now.

Ben clicked the cart in place and turned to me. "You're a pretty girl. You could get out of your poor town if you behaved like a proper lady." He looked me up and down, at my simple handstitched gown and leather boots, my satchel swung across my body, and my wild hair tucked into one of Mama's scarves. Even though I lived with a seamstress, we usually made our own clothes from leftover fabric—which meant patchwork dresses and mismatched stockings. Still, Mr. Ben Jones didn't seem displeased with my appearance. He licked his spitty lips and took a deep breath, like he just realized I was indeed a woman and not some dirty peasant girl.

He said, "A good bath and a silken dress—you'd pass as a real lady as long as you kept your mouth shut. I can think of a few wealthy men who'd love to have you."

And just like that, my sadness turned to anger. "I may not be able to go to school, but I will find a way to earn my keep—maybe even get wealthy someday. And it won't be because I married some rich man. I'll get rich because I earned it. Because *God* gave it to me!" I stomped my foot when I was done.

Ben just climbed onto his horse, as graceful as a prince, and looked down at me as he said, "Until then, you'll be nothing more than a peasant girl who rode in on a donkey and who's leaving on a donkey. You should be happy I even offered my advice."

"I don't need your advice."

"But you do need my money." He dropped a leather pouch on the ground in front of me. "That'll cover everything."

I stepped aside so he could pass and watched the cart until I couldn't see it anymore. I didn't touch the pouch of money until he was gone.

***

Since the sun was still high, I decided to take a trip through the woods and find the scribal house Ben had mentioned. Ruby and I walked for an hour before we reached a clearing in the trail. I didn't want to get too close and risk being seen, so I tied Ruby to a tree and took the hard path—through the shrubbery.

After a while, I saw a house. Not a shack like what I lived in, but an actual house with multiple stories and an enclosed porch and *two* chimneys. I was so mesmerized by it; I hadn't noticed I'd stood from the brush and walked into the clearing. Suddenly, a man opened the front door and frowned at me.

"Miss, are you lost?"

I gasped. "I'm just looking. A Scribe named Ben Jones told me I could visit."

"Ben Jones?" His face twisted. "He's not a Scribe."

Now I was frowning. "He's not?"

"He's just my apprentice. That fool lies so much he can't possibly be a Scribe. But this *is* a house, not a museum, so you must—" the door flung open and released a frantic young man.

"Mr. Marlowe, pages are missing from most of these stories!" He was holding a stack of books in his hands, piled so high he had to tilt his chin up to shout over them. "One book is missing a lot! What are we going to do?"

"Which book?" The old man turned and rushed into the house, slamming the door behind him. I wanted to leave, but something inside wouldn't let me. I snuck around the back of the house and found an open window, keeping low so no one would see me snooping.

Inside, I could hear the frantic man saying, "This one is missing an *incredible* amount. All I can tell from the fading text is that there was a man who was strong enough to win battles on his own. And the battle was with the Trojans, I think."

"That's no good. We can't bring these great stories to life if part of the story is missing." The older man sounded just as frantic now. "We'll have to make it up. We've got to come up with *something* in order to tell this story."

"But what?" the young man asked. "What kind of story is about a man fighting a war, whose weakness is the tendon in his heel? How do we explain why his heel is his weakness? What kind of a name can we even give to man like that?"

Heavy footsteps approached the window, my cue to sprint for the forest. I ran without looking back.

* * *

When I returned home, I took the money right to Mr. Hemmindale. He counted the coins as I rattled on about all the beautiful things I saw in that great city. He held up a silver coin and inspected it, then moved on to the next. I stopped talking; there were dozens of silver coins in the bag, and when he finally got to the bottom, he pulled out a handful of gold coins and something he called, "paper money."

"I hate paper money," he grunted. "I can't use it here because no one around here even knows what it is!" Mr. Hemmindale's face was red. He looked over at me. "Did he give you any tips?"

"No, sir," I said quickly.

He pinched the bridge of his nose. "I can't use this money. Now I'll be set back on orders. What am I gonna do?" He lowered his head.

"You'll make it, Mr. Hemminale. We always do, don't we?"

He sniffled. "You're right." He counted out a few of the coins. "Since he didn't tip you, I'll give you a little extra."

I held up my hands. "Mr. Hemmindale, I can go back and get you the coins you wanted. I'm a merchant, I know how important it is to have the right coins to bargain with. It's no big deal for me. Besides, I'd love to see that beautiful town again."

Mr. Hemmindale looked shocked. "I don't know what to say. I can't ask you to go back there, and I won't have the money to pay you for a second trip."

"You didn't ask; I volunteered. So don't worry about the pay." I shrugged. "I really want to see that town again, and if this is a way I can do it, I'd love to go for you."

Mr. Hemmindale stood and hugged me. "Thank you so much, Amana."

"You're welcome, Mr. Hemmindale. I'll come by tomorrow morning."

He pulled away and pressed a few coins into my palm. "I'll give you the rest of your payment when you get back." I opened my palm and stared at the two gold triangles in my hand. The gold shined so brightly; I'd never seen one up close before. This was my very first gold coin.

"No way," I whispered breathlessly.

Mr. Hemmindale laughed. "You earned it. And when you come back, there'll be more where that came from."

Without thinking, I hugged him once more and then ran to Ruby, shouting goodbye over my shoulder. I needed to see Ray.

The Castillos shack was smaller than mine. It had only one small doorway, while I had two. The shack itself sat on stones, keeping it from flooding on rainy days. They didn't have a porch at all, you just hopped up the stacked stones and walked through the creaky door. Most summer days, they didn't even have a door, just some animal skins hanging over the doorway. During the winter months, they tied some wooden planks together and propped it up to keep the wind and snow out. I always knew we all lived hard, but I never knew *how* hard until I visited that fancy town.

"Ray!" I called from outside. I heard some movement and finally Ray appeared. His dark hair was sitting on his shoulders, and he held his shirt in his hand as he peeped out the doorway.

"I'm back," I grinned.

He stepped outside. "That was a long trip. Did you like it?"

"I loved it! I'm going again tomorrow."

"What?"

For some reason, his frown made me want to explain. "They messed up the order or something like that. I told Mr. Hemmindale I would go again so I could get the rest of the money he's owed."

"You can't go." He shook his head. "There's too many orders you could miss tomorrow."

"I'm not gonna miss any orders. I'll have Ma go to the market for me."

"What about your Pa?"

"It's alright for him to be alone for a few hours, Ray. And I want to see that city again. I have to."

Ray put his hands on his hips and said, "Fine. But I'm going with you this time."

"Don't you have to help at your tent? Your mother is pregnant."

"I'm sure my parents can handle things on their own."

I chewed my lip. "I don't know."

"You shouldn't travel alone anyway. And I want to see this magical city." He rolled his eyes and put on his shirt.

I'd wanted to tell Ray every little detail about that place; it was great that he wanted to come along. I don't know why I was fighting him, so I nodded and said, "Alright, Ray. Meet me at Mr. Hemmindale's tomorrow."

"Good. I'll ride my donkey so you can ride in the cart. Ruby might be too tired for a second trip."

"She'll be fine," I said. "Besides I don't want to stare at the back of your head all day, riding in the cart."

Ray laughed, running a hand through his hair. "My head doesn't look that bad."

I quirked an eyebrow. "You haven't seen the back of your head."

"You'll get to see more of the city if you're not worried about Ruby."

"That's true," I paused. "Fine. I'll ride in the cart."

He grinned. "Good."

"You'll have to dress nice."

"Fancy place, huh?" He flicked his eyes away, like he was picturing the town in his head.

"It's like everything we ever dreamed, Ray."

His eyes glittered in the fading sunlight. "I'll dress as nice as I can."

When I arrived at my shack, I tied Ruby to the wooden fence out front and left her a bucket of food while I went to fetch her water from the well. It was a ten-minute walk all the way there and the whole time I thought of the story of the great warrior from the Trojan war. The man was invincible, except for his one weakness—a tendon in his heel. *What a strange weak spot,* I thought.

As I lowered the pale into the well, I wondered how the original writer came to think of such a story. *How would he be invincible everywhere on his body except his heel?* As I pulled the pale back up, I noticed the handle wasn't wet. It's usually left dry because you never completely submerge the pale in the water below, only enough to be filled with water. Any deeper and the handle would be too wet and slippery to carry. I stared at the pale, watching the water slosh around inside, and for a second, I believed I had a story.

"What if," I said aloud, "what if the mighty warrior was dipped in a well of some sort that made him invincible? That would be better." I hurried up getting that water back to Ruby so I could tell her my ideas.

"It wouldn't make sense for the warrior to just walk into the water right, Ruby? If he did that, then he would've gotten his heel wet and he wouldn't have a weak spot at all. But who would dip him?" I rubbed her as she drank, lapping up the water like she was thirsty as all heck. "I kind of like the dipping idea. Don't you?"

"Don't you what?" Ma called.

I turned around and smiled at my mother. "Nothin',

Ma. I'm just talking to Ruby."

She extended her arms as I climbed the porch steps, waiting for a bear hug. "How was your trip?" she asked.

"It was great, Mother." I took a step back. "You look amazing." She had on a yellow dress she'd made herself. It made her dark skin look so vibrant and beautiful, even made her look more energetic, instead of tired and dull.

She laughed and sashayed inside, going straight to the pot she had cooking over the fire. "What do you want, child?"

"Oh, come on, Ma. Can't I just give you a compliment? You are my mama after all." She was right, though. I was trying to butter her up so I could ask her to work the market tomorrow.

"I know you, Ms. Favian, and you are always up to something." Mother turned to face me. She was smiling today; it was refreshing. I instantly regretted agreeing to go on the trip for Mr. Hemmindale, but it was too late now.

"Mama," I sighed. I walked over and grabbed the fire poker and tended to the flames as she sat down in her rocking chair. "I did something selfish." Behind me, she'd started knitting on one of her orders. "I told Mr. Hemmindale I would go back to the city tomorrow. But Ray is going to go with me and he's better with directions than I am, so I'm sure the trip won't be so long." The black cast iron pot sat bubbling over the fire. It was the only noise, paired with the creaking of Ma's chair.

I stood there for a minute waiting for her to respond; when she didn't, I said, "I just wanted to help Mr. Hemmindale. Now you'll have to go to the market tomorrow. It all happened so fast, but I—"

"You were right, Amana, you were selfish. This isn't even about Mr. Hemmindale, is it?"

"Yes, it is. Partially." I fiddled around for my coin purse and pulled out the two gold coins. "We got two gold callios, and Mr. Hemmindale said he could give us even more after this trip!" Mother stopped knitting. She looked up at me finally, but her face was not pleasant. Her eyebrows were low, and her strong jaw was clenched tight. Mother was tall, but in that moment, she seemed like a giant. She walked up to me and stared me straight in the eye. Her eyes flicked down at the triangles in my hand and all at once, anger clouded her face. She smacked the coins from my hand and threw me to the floor.

"You think this is about money? You think getting more money is gonna help us?"

I rolled over and tried to get away. Ma lost her temper some days, and often she lost it on me. But she was so tired and under so much stress, I never blamed her for the beatings. I crawled backwards from her, fumbling for words.

"I thought we'd be able to pay for Pa's medicine if we got more money!"

She snatched me by the collar of my dress and pulled me up so she could look me in the eye. Her face was so close I could smell her breath. "You think money will help? People don't help us because we are nothing but poor rubbish that fancy folk ain't sure what to do with no more. Money won't fix your father and it won't fix your foolishness, either. Have I taught you nothing?"

I tried to stay calm, but my heart was racing, and my breathing was out of control. Ragged breaths ran from my lips as I stared at Ma, watching all the sanity leave her eyes. I'd seen her like this before, it was like she was a different person. Anything could set her off now.

She frowned—worse than the scowling she'd already been doing. "You know I hate that panicky breathing. Stop it!" she yelled.

I held my breath. But I was still dangling in front of her, her fist gripping my collar. I couldn't calm down and I couldn't hold my breath forever. The panic kept coming. Bubbling inside me just like the soup in the cast iron pot. My mother was the flames, and *everything* was the poker.

Her thick arm lashed out and she grabbed my throat. I started flailing. I scratched and reached for anything, my gaze never leaving Mother's tired eyes. They looked so angry, but I knew she wasn't really mad. She was tired and stressed, and I'm sure she didn't mean to hurt me. But she *was* hurting me and there was nothing I could do, except wait until the episode passed.

I wished I could stop flailing, to show her I would do anything for her. I knew it would be easier for my parents if I wasn't around. There would be more money, more food, and Ma wouldn't have to work so hard. I wanted to give in to the weakness I felt, drowning out all my thoughts. But for some reason, my body kept fighting. I thrashed in the air, jerking from the lack of oxygen, desperately clinging to my retreating consciousness.

Finally, my vision started to blur, and I wondered, as I faded, if I could ever come up with a name for the great immortal warrior. It's strange, the last thing I wanted to do before I died was finish that story I'd overheard the Scribes discussing earlier. I didn't want to say goodbye to Ray, didn't want to help out Mr. Hemmindale one last time. All I wanted was to write down my thoughts and hope that someone else would read them.

Darkness blotted out the last bit of light left in my world. Ma's angry eyes was the last thing I saw before it all went black. In the distance of this void, I heard a loud noise and a voice that sounded familiar. I felt my mother's hands release me. But I was too weak to breathe; so I laid there and drifted away.

Chapter Three
The Gold Rush

When I woke up, I didn't recognize the room I was in. I sat up quickly in bed and glanced around. *Where am I?* There wasn't much in the room, just a few pairs of pants on a chair, some neatly folded shirts on the floor, and knickknacks laying around—obviously a boy's room.

Someone knocked on the door. I placed a hand to my throat and croaked out, "Come in."

It was Ray, wearing a plain shirt and dirty trousers with patches on the knees. "How are you?" He closed the door and sat on the corner of the bed while I stared at the floor. "Your mother, uh, you guys were fighting again. It got kind of bad."

I nodded.

"You remember anything?"

"Not really."

"I was coming over to see if I could borrow one of your Pa's clean shirts for the trip. Ruby was going crazy out front and there was shouting inside. I went in and pulled your mother off of you. She was ..." he paused to shake his head. "She was choking you, Amana. Even though you were already passed out. Even though you weren't even moving anymore. She was still choking you."

I shifted, fisting the blankets to keep from covering my ears. I didn't want to hear any of this, but I had to. If Ray could handle seeing me like that then I could handle hearing him tell it.

"I started doing some compressions on you, but I wasn't sure if it was working. I thought you were dead. But you're stronger than that." He sniffled, turning so I couldn't see his face anymore. "You came back to me, Amana. Coughing and vomiting, but you were back. My dad came over and calmed Ma down, checked on your father. My mother got you cleaned up and changed your clothes."

He turned to me, a weak smile on his trembling lips. "She hit you pretty good, right there." Ray touched my forehead and it stung. I squinted and winced at the pain.

"That hurts."

"She must have knocked your head loose. You kept mumbling a name in your sleep."

"What name?"

He ruffled his loose hair. "Achilles."

"Oh," I whispered.

Ray stared at me; his eyes looked defeated. "Why do you stay with her? It's happening more and more now."

"She's my *mother*. I can't let her take care of Pa alone."

Ray clenched his jaw and closed his eyes. For some reason, I wanted to cry. But not for me. I wanted to cry for him. He cared but he didn't understand. He never would because his mother was healthy, and his dad wasn't confined to his bed. The most Ray had to worry about was finding a pretty wife, and it wasn't like he didn't have women lining up at his tent as volunteers. But I didn't hate him or blame him for that. Ray was upset because he cared.

I scooted to the edge of the bed and grabbed his hand. "Thank you for saving me again." Ray pulled me close and hugged me tight.

"Here." He let go and passed me my coin bag.

I opened it up and saw the two gold coins from Mr. Hemmindale, plus a handful of silvers and coppers. My head snapped up to Ray and he explained, "The money from the market. I sold as much as I could, plus I picked up a few orders for the winter. I don't know if your mother will be able to get to them after last night, but…" he sighed.

"Thank you, Ray," I said, closing the pouch.

"I found the gold coins on the floor of your shack when I ran in to help. Snatched them up so fast," he stopped to chuckle, "I'd never seen a gold coin before."

"You could've left them for Ma." I shrugged. "She'll need them more than I will."

"She doesn't need money. She needs help."

"She's just tired, Ray."

"How long are you going to make excuses for her? Last time you wore bruises for a month. You can't go back there. I won't let you."

"You don't get to control me. Even if it comes from a place of concern." I patted his hand. "I'll be fine. Once I become a ..." I trailed off, gazing out the window at the sunrise. "We're late!" I yelled, scrambling off the bed but Ray grabbed my arm.

"Amana, we're not going."

"We are." I wrenched my arm free. "We have to."

"You are in no state to travel."

"I don't care—"

"Amana!"

"Ray!" I threw my hands into the air. "I have to make a better life for my family. I can't lose this chance." Before he could reply, I turned and left, walking barefoot through the shack.

"Amana, wait!" Ray chased after me, but I was already out the front door and on my way back to my home.

"Is this even about helping Mr. Hemmindale?" Ray called.

"No," I said back. "Not anymore."

I went inside and shut the door behind me, moving quietly through the house. Shy rays of sunlight peeped through the tattered curtains to punch holes of light into the dark living room. Ma's rocking chair was flipped over and broken, her knitting needles thrown across the room. The fire had died out, and the food smelled burned.

I ignored the mess and ghosted through the shack, collecting things for the trip. Hard cheese and sausage, crusts of stale bread, a clean dress, stockings, and a scarf for my head. My shoes were at the door, a worn pair of leather boots I'd had for years. Part of me wanted to peek into Ma and Pa's room but I was afraid of making too much noise, so I ignored their room and stood by the front door. I said a prayer before I left, asking God to protect them while I was gone and maybe calm Ray's anger so he wouldn't hate me for this. For the first time in a very long time, I felt at peace. As I stood there asking God to look over me, I couldn't ignore the sense that I was finally doing something with my life. This trip wasn't about me at all—or Mr. Hemmindale or Ma. It was bigger than I imagined, like God Himself was sitting up there on His throne tellin' me to go on and make a difference in this world. *I am with you.*

With a shiver, I whispered, "In Jesus' name, amen." Then I went outside, untied Ruby from the fence, and got ready to leave.

"C'mon, girl. We've got to at least try." I saddled her up and climbed on. As we made our way down the hill and past the Castillo shack, I saw Ray waiting at the bottom of the hill with his own donkey. He'd changed into a fresh shirt, and trousers without patches. His hair was slicked back, and he wore a jerkin that was a little too small.

When I got close, he said, "I promised I'd go. So my mom will run your tent today. But you've gotta promise me two things."

"What things?"

"When we get back, you'll at least consider staying with us some days."

I nodded.

"And you gotta tell me what 'Achilles' means." That shy smile of his cracked his face; the sight of it instantly shifted the mood in the air.

I laughed and said, "Are you sure you wanna know?"

"I've been dying to know."

As we rode together, I explained everything to Ray. The School of Knowledge, the scribal house, even the story I'd overheard and how I'd been thinking of a name for the main character.

"Apparently, I figured out the name without even knowing. I'm going to call him Achilles."

Ray scratched the back of his head. "That's a weird weakness. And an even weirder name."

"How?"

"Because," he paused, trying to think of the right words. "I don't know much about books and science and stuff, but I'm pretty sure Achilles is a part of our body. It's weird to name your character after a body part—especially since that's his weakness."

I shook my head. "No—don't you remember what Ben Jones said? We can change history."

He cocked his head to the side. "Is it '*we*' already?"

"You know what I mean." I sighed. "The Scribes rewrite stories all the time. They can alter history and make it seem like the Achilles tendon is a term that came from my story. Not the other way around."

He thought about this a moment, then nodded slowly. "I get it. But if you do change the name, you should name him something cooler."

"Cooler?" I squinted.

He grinned. "How about, Mighty Guy?"

"That's the stupidest name ever," I snorted. "I think I'll stick with Achilles. But on our way into the town, I want to buy paper and ink so I can write down my ideas."

"For what?"

I looked him straight in the eye. "To give to one of the men from the school." Ray shook his head, but I wouldn't let him talk me out of it. "I know it's dangerous, but I've got to do this, Ray. It isn't about money or even about Ma anymore. I ..." I paused because I knew I was about to sound crazy. "I know God is telling me to do this. I feel it in my bones, Ray. Like the Holy Spirit won't let this fire burn out."

Ray sat quiet. Most poor folk didn't know how to read. We didn't go to school or even leave our small town often. But we did go to church together. The Scribes might be able to alter history, but they would never alter our beliefs. So when I saw Ray give a slow nod and exhale a big sigh, I knew he was on my side.

We stopped by the nearby town to grab paper and ink. It cost me 5 silver callios, but the paper was thick and creamy, and the ink was imported from a foreign country. I wanted this letter to be perfect, in the hopes that maybe things wouldn't go awry.

"Are you sure this is worth it?" Ray asked as he sat under a tree beside me. He took a big bite from the hard cheese I'd packed and reached for the sausage.

I didn't look up at him as I dipped my pen into the ink pot. "This way is safer than just walking in and announcing I'm a Scribe. If I write a properly structured letter in an uncommon, formal language, they'll know I'm a woman who knows her stuff. I'm not going to ask for enrollment, I'm just asking them to consider my revisions to the Achilles story. And I'm writing the letter in Arabic—a language I'd have no way to learn without my Gift."

"What if they sum it all up to insanity? Or witchcraft?" Ray asked between bites.

"I'm writing two letters. One for the scribal school, and the other I'll deliver to a newspaper service."

Ray packed the food away, wiped some grease from the sausage off his face, and said, "You must want to die."

"Going public will get a better response."

"Or a public execution."

"I thought you were supporting me in this," I said angrily.

"I am. Which is why I'm making sure you check every option. The newspapers aren't going to consider anything written from a woman. Especially not if you're calling out a scribal school. There's only four in existence! They're gonna read that letter and come hang you."

"You're wrong," I said, scribbling down my letter. He had to be.

"You got a way to escape certain death?"

"I don't have to tell them my name." I hadn't even thought of that until the words left my mouth. Ray was looking at me but not like he disagreed, he was shocked— which meant this was a good idea. I kept going. "I'm not going to write under my middle name, I'll use my first name. And when I go to submit the letters, I'll pretend I'm just a mail carrier for the real author. But I'll sign my full name on the copy for the scribal school."

"What about your last name?" Ray asked slowly.

"No one from our poor town would ever think anyone in the newspapers would be related to us."

"That's true." He leaned back in the grass, tugging my long braid as he said my full name. "Favian Amana Hart."

The tugging was messing up my writing, so I pulled my hair away and reached for the scarf I'd packed. Most women my color weren't allowed to have our hair out in public anyway, but I'd let it out because the sun had been so violently hot, I was sweatin' grease.

Ray watched me tuck my hair away, his eyes glowing even in the shade. "First thing you alter when you become a Scribe is the law that makes you hide your hair."

"Does that mean you believe I'll become a Scribe?"

"It means I believe your plan just might work."

"I'm gonna get us out of our small town and into this fancy one. We're not gonna be poor anymore, Ray."

Ray and I sat silently under the tree a while longer as I wrote out both letters. I took my time with each stroke. I didn't want to write sloppily, and I'd never used such expensive ink before. After I finished, I placed the letters in a fine leather covering to keep them straight. Clenching both letters, I prayed for favor from God, that He would allow this plan to work. When I finished praying, I collected my things and hopped onto Ruby. Ray followed right behind me, and we rode in silence to the bridge leading into town.

"Are you ready to see what's past these gates?" I asked Ray as we got closer.

"Of course," he said nervously.

When we finally passed the gates, Ray remained quiet, but his silence didn't fool me. I saw the way his eyes trailed the finely dressed men and women walking by; the young children dressed better than even the richest in our town. Everything was better the second time for me, but Ray seemed distant, lost in his head just like the time we rode down to Mr. Hemmindale's farm. He clenched his jaw, almost as if he was angry. I left him alone, we had things to do, and I wasn't going to let Ray's moodiness get us off track.

"There's a newspaper place right up here," I said to Ray. "I can see if they'll have my letter." I hopped off Ruby and passed him the reins, ignoring his scowl.

The entrance was guarded by massive doors of stained glass. I grunted as I pushed them open.

"Disgusting!" a woman complained inside.

I glanced around as I pushed through the door,

wondering about the trouble, but I quickly realized the woman was talking about me. Every eye in the shop was staring right at me.

"Can I help you?" An older Black man approached me. He wore silver rimmed glasses and a shirt so white it put shame to the coming winter snow. I gave him a thin smile as he stood before me, noticing the way the other customers watched him expectantly. Then it hit me; this man was the owner of this shop.

"I'd like to have this letter posted in the newspaper." I thrusted it at him, keeping my eyes on the wooden floor as the room began to murmur.

"I can't just put anything in the paper, I need to know it's worth printing costs."

I looked up at him. "It is worth it. I think I may have found a new Scribe."

All the murmuring became hisses.

The man leaned toward me. "It's best you go back to where you came from before you get yourself in trouble up here."

I frowned. *Go back to where I came from*. By the looks of things, him and I came from the same place. Only difference was his fancy clothes. But I realized, as he stood there with his arms crossed and the other customers snickering behind him, that we couldn't be any more different. He was exactly like all those fancy folks with their silk scarves and lace gloves, pearl necklaces, and gold pocket watches. I was the odd one out and it wasn't 'cause of my cocoa skin.

The man said, "These folks don't take witchcraft and scribal hypocrisy lightly."

"Neither do I." I slammed the letter down on the wooden table beside us. I wasn't going to let my ugly dress and torn stockings stop me from accomplishing this mission.

The man shook his grey head. "You don't wanna play with me, girl."

I could feel my palms become slick with sweat, but I didn't want to cower. Ray and I had come too far, and God wouldn't let me walk away from this. I was meant to be here, and I wasn't going to let some old man and snobby rich folk stop me.

"I *ain't* playing," I said. "Now it's best you open this letter and give it a fair reading before you start making accusations."

"Is that a threat?" He leaned down so he could look me in the eye.

I leaned in, too, ignoring my trembling hands. We were so close; I could feel his coffee breath on my face. "Read the letter," I said plainly.

"I ain't reading it. You can't afford to have something printed in my papers."

I dropped a gold coin on the table, right on top of my letter. I wanted to tell him how he was wrong and how he didn't know me well enough to tell me what I could afford, but the open-mouthed look on his face let me know he'd already realized that. Triumphant, I turned and left to meet Ray outside.

"You alright?" he asked as I wobbled out on shaky legs.

"I was so nervous!" I gasped. My chest hurt so bad, I thought I was havin' a heart attack.

"You see why I wanted the cart?" Ray asked, helping me into Ruby's saddle.

I gripped her reins. "I guess."

We rode to the edge of city in silence until we reached the start of the forest. "We have to walk the rest of the way," I said, hopping down from Ruby.

"Really?" Ray asked,

"It's the only way to the house."

Ray thought a moment, then said, "I'll stay here."

"You don't want to see the house?"

"I do, but I've got a weird feeling about this."

"Don't tell me you're scared." I smirked.

He shook his head. "I'm telling you, something's not right."

"Fine, I'll go on my own."

Ray stayed with the donkeys as I wandered into the forest

alone again. I followed the path along the ground to find the work of art that Ben had went on about. The house was definitely nice, but I hadn't seen enough works of art to compare it to.

As I walked through the brush, I thought hard on what I should say to the men when I arrived, but my thoughts were cut short when I heard someone call out, "Who's there? Show yourself!"

I walked out of the bushes with my hands held up. Ben Jones stood there holding a rifle at me.

"Please don't shoot. I'm just here to trade this money. Mr. Hemmindale said he can't use paper money. He needs all coins."

Ben said, "You're the filthy peasant from yesterday." He lowered the gun with a sigh, and I dropped to my knees, exhausted from the tension.

"Sorry for just showing up. Mr. Hemmindale really needed the money," I offered.

Ben glared down at me. "Get up. I'll trade the monies inside."

I followed him to the house, but just as I stepped inside, he turned and slammed door so fast it hit my foot with a *thud!*

"Ouch!" I cried, stepping back.

Ben unlatched the door viewer, there was just enough room to see the smirk on his face. "Peasants are not allowed inside the house. Please wait here." Then he turned and left.

I could have stayed there and tended to my sore foot, but my curiosity was swelling. When I thought Ben was far enough away, I reached through the door viewer, unlocked the door, and limped into the house.

I had no time to marvel at the clean floors or the bookshelves tall enough to scrape the ceilings. As soon as I stepped inside, I began opening doors and cabinets looking for a good place to leave my letter. There didn't seem to be a good spot in the first room, so I rounded the corner to the next ... and came face to face with Ben Jones.

A heartbeat of surprise ticked by as he blinked in confusion. Then he recognized who I was and realized I'd snuck into the house. His face curdled in anger and his lip curled up as he started to shout, but I turned and ran before he could get the words out.

Ben was right behind me, shouting as I limped as fast as I could. I found a room with a sturdy door and ducked inside, slamming it in his face.

"You filthy peasant! What do you think you're doing in here? Stealing all the gold! And here I thought you were an honest peasant! You are filth just like the rest of them! Now open the door!"

He pounded on the door with each word, but I had locked it before he could fiddle with the handle. I wasted no time, limping through the room, searching for an exit. There was a pathway in the back that led into the hallway again. I tiptoed through, listening for Ben, making sure he was still outside the door.

When I was safe again, I found a small room in the house. There was nothing in it but a wooden table with a matching chair. There were papers scattered about the small round table. I felt through them, reading quickly. Then I found leatherbound folders stuffed with pages. One was labeled, *Henry VI* and another, *Unfinished Works*. I glossed over some of the pages in the *Unfinished Works* folder, reading all the different titles. *Leashing My Shrewish Wife* and *Dr. Faustus*.

The titles seemed silly, but the way the words dazzled on the page made me want to read more. *Henry VI* seemed the most finished. I grabbed that piece and tucked it under my arm. Outside, I could hear Ben stomping through the house. He must have realized I'd given him the slip.

I gingerly placed my letter on the table, atop all of the papers. And as I turned to leave, I noticed a small wooden box on the corner of the table. The box was unlatched and slightly open, but I could still see the beautiful tree carved into the lid. Quietly, I reached over and opened it, gold coins stared back at me. I wanted to take the whole box, but there was no place for me to hide it, so I grabbed a big handful and filled my purse strapped around my waist. I knew it was stealing, but I figured Ben probably wouldn't pay me now.

With my purse stuffed full, I crept to the door and placed my ear against it, listening for Ben. It'd gotten quiet out in the halls, no more yelling or stomping around. A spidery chill tiptoed down my spine; Ben was probably listening for me as well. I didn't want to risk bumping into him again, so I crossed the small room and stood in front of a window. It was small but so was I, and I was running out of options. Wiping nervous sweat from my forehead, I opened the window and dropped my bundle of stories to the ground, then climbed out as quickly as I could, scraping my left leg on the way down.

I groaned as I lay on the ground but there was no time to focus on the pain. As soon as I got to my feet, I heard footsteps coming towards me.

"There you are!" I heard Ben yell.

Without thinking, I grabbed my papers and dashed for the forest. The air shattered beside me, and a hissing noise screamed in my ear. I covered my ears and dived to the ground, crawling on my belly as another round went off. The shots were loud, but they weren't close to me; the tree to my left shattered and then one further away exploded as a bullet went through it. *He doesn't know where I'm at*, I thought. So I took off again, balling up my dress and running for dear life.

I stepped on rocks and pebbles, soft ground and coarse blades of grass, all with trees exploding around me. But I kept moving, I had to or else I'd be explodin' next.

The clearing came into view, which meant Ray was somewhere nearby. "Ray! Ray!" I screamed. He didn't respond. Another shot hissed like a preying snake, forcing my legs to go faster.

"RAY! WE GOTTA RUN! *RUN!*"

As I burst from the trees, I tripped over a root and hit the ground. I quickly recovered, but I still couldn't find Ray. Just as the air beside me shattered like thunder, I heard his voice cry out, "Amana! Over here!" Ray had hidden under some trees, but he was coming now with Ruby and his donkey.

"We gotta go!" I jumped onto Ruby, and we took off.

Ruby loved to run for fun, but I knew she couldn't run for long. So, I avoided the town traffic and cut through the woods, straight for the bridge. The closer we got to the bridge the less hissing I heard until, finally, we didn't hear anything at all.

"What happened back there?" Ray demanded. We had crossed the bridge and were far enough away to speak openly.

"The guy almost broke my foot." I couldn't face his angry eyes, so I kept my eyes on Ruby, patting the top of her head. "I got an idea, and I just went with it. It was an impulse decision."

"What kind of an impulse decision did you make, Amana?" Ray's voice was low. His words were so sharp, I actually began to twitch.

"He wouldn't let me in, so I found my own way in."

"Are you serious? I told you this was a bad idea. Something was wrong, I told you!"

"I know but look what I got." I unfolded the papers with the story, 'Henry VI' on it.

"You stole some of their stories?" Ray's face was distorted in anger.

"I'm just borrowing it," I said. "I needed a little leverage in case they want to do something rash. Now I can bargain with them."

He shook his head. "You're not thinking straight. They SHOT at you! There's no bargaining with them!"

"I don't know if they'll kill me for that."

"For *that*?" his voice cracked. "As in, there's something else?"

I unstrapped my purse and opened it. "I took these. But only because I didn't think we would be able to get the correct payment from Ben"

Ray stared at the gold.

"Ray, say something."

"Get off your donkey right now," he snapped.

"Why?"

"Just get off."

We got off our donkeys and stood in a field of flowers. Ray walked over to me and looked in my purse. "How much paper money did he have?"

"I don't know," I shrugged. "Not much, maybe two or three sheets of paper."

Ray put his hand on my back and pulled me close to him. It was so sudden and so different from the way we'd ever hugged before—not like when I'd just woken up from Ma's beating or the time I sprained my ankle and he carried me home a few months back. This was different and it left my heart fluttering.

"Ray, back up," I said.

"Amana, you're rich." He pulled away and stared at me. His skin was radiant, and his eyes smiled on their own. "You definitely have enough to pay Mr. Hemmindale, make a payment to yourself, tip yourself, and still have a grand chunk of change. Amana, you did it!" Ray lifted me into the air and hugged me tight.

"Ray," I breathed, hugging him back. "This is only the beginning. These people are going to come looking for me, and when they do, I'll really be something. This money is nothing compared to what I'm about to get."

Ray pulled away, frowning. He set me back on my feet and said, "Here we go again. Amana, sweetheart, you're *rich*! You don't have to try to become a Scribe anymore.

You're set!"

"Did you really think I wanted to become a Scribe to gain social status and money?"

He opened his mouth and then shut it.

"I'm becoming a Scribe because it's my calling. Because all the women who died before me need someone to make their deaths worth it. Because God is telling me to make a difference in this world!"

Ray flopped down on the ground and covered his face. "You are the dumbest person I know. I don't know why I'm ... never mind."

"You're what?"

"I'm tired," he huffed. "Let's just go home."

Chapter Four
Let Go

Quite some time passed since I'd left the letter at the scribal house. I anxiously waited for news every day, but nothing came. As time dragged on, defeat began to weigh on me, but I knew there was some buzz going around about someone named Favian Hart. It had even made it all the way back to my little town—but what stunned me the most is that the gossip started on the other side of town, nowhere near the fancy scribal city.

Word around the block was that whoever published that letter must be a Scribe. Single women swooned over him, fanning themselves at the thought of a rich young Scribe somewhere near town. They made up stories about how handsome he was; probably tall, dark skinned, and definitely educated. I always giggled when I saw girls squealing over Favian, little did they know, *she* was right beside them.

After the scribal incident, I stopped doing runs for Mr. Hemmindale. I told him I would need a bit of time off to help my mother. It wasn't a lie, I did need to help Ma, but I also wanted things to cool down at the scribal house. After being shot at by Ben Jones, I had no idea how any real Scribe would react to seeing me. So I stayed away.

Those days in town seemed more distant as time inched forward. They weren't quite memories, but they'd begun to fade from my mind, beaten away by the hazy sun, by afternoon chores, by long hours at the market. There was too much in the present for me to focus on, I didn't have time for the past. But I fought to hold on to those memories when I couldn't feel that electricity from before. All that excitement, determination, the whispers of God running over my skin. I wouldn't let myself forget those things. Even if it seemed like I didn't have time for any thoughts outside of making a good deal, my foot—sore from having Ben slam it in the doorway—always reminded me of that day.

Although I told Mr. Hemmindale I couldn't run deliveries for a while, I never really got the chance to tell that to my mother. She and I barely spoke after that night. It was best that way, so we could avoid fighting. Since we didn't speak much, I never told her about all the gold coins, either. I spent my nights wandering through town, looking for clues for the meaning behind the story I'd stolen. I'd never heard of a 'play' before, only great stories, or tales of champions and gods.

I would spend my time at the nicest place in town, the Literature of the Scribes. It was a brick building that held different works from Scribes of the past. Every town and city had to have one. Inside the museum you could see a few pieces on display, samples of work from past Scribes, a few unfinished books, a Bible, and two dictionaries. I browsed the works of the past Scribes, but I didn't find any clues until I decided to look up the word 'play' in one of the dictionaries. The older dictionary described the word as having a "Middle English pleien from Old English plegian" origin, and that the word meant to move lightly and quickly, to rejoice, to amuse oneself. The newer dictionary copied over by the latest Scribe, Christopher Marlowe, contained a description with more detail; frolic, mock, to perform. Neither of the definitions made much sense to me.

As I read through Henry VI, I noticed the formatting was different from any book I'd ever seen. There were descriptions on the side of the pages that explained how the characters felt, what facial expression they should be making. There was even something called 'staging' written on the page. There was detail on where people should stand when they read through the play. The conversations were easy to understand, but I wanted there to be more to it. So, I decided not to write any more until I could understand what I was reading.

As I prayed day and night about what it meant to write a play, God finally answered me. Eventually, I'd decided to go back working for Mr. Hemmindale again, and went to visit him after the market closed.

"Hello? Mr. Hemmindale?" I heard a door open and close.

He called, "Yes? Who's there?"

"It's me, Amana!" He didn't answer until he stepped into the lit barn.

"Amana? What are you doing here?" Mr. Hemmindale looked incredible. He wasn't wearing his usual straw hat and stressed face. His beard was trimmed, and his skin looked smooth like porcelain, instead of red and burned from long days in the sun. His brows and his hair had been tamed somehow—there was no hair growing down his neck. His jaw looked chiseled and strong, and his figure was pronounced in the fitted clothes he wore.

I'd never seen Mr. Hemmindale look so stunning. His black stockings were covered by beautiful high boots. They were leather and had a shine like I'd never seen before. His overcoat was striped with reds and yellows while gold chains connected one side of the coat to the other. On his shoulder was a golden brooch that held a short cloak made from moose skin and lined with a lush velvet red so intense I couldn't look away. Mr. Hemmindale looked just like the rich men from the town of Sesame, where Ben Jones lived.

"Mr. Hemmindale, is that you?"

The finely dressed man laughed and said, "Of course! I know the getup may be a little outlandish for an old farmer like me. But tonight is a special night, ya' see. My late wife used to be part of the theatre life; she performed in plays and was rather good. I reckon that's how most rich folks meet their spouse, running into someone at a play."

"Wait ... a *play*? What is that?" I could hardly believe Mr. Hemmindale's appearance, let alone that he knew what a play was.

"Ahh yes, you folk around here have never seen nothing like that, I bet. Theatre isn't a real big thing here in this town. But where the rich folks live, they get to see the plays whenever they want—with the best scripts, too! Most plays are just a way for the writer to sorta say what he always wanted to say, but with other people saying it for him."

"Um, I don't think I understand that."

"Well, it's like I said earlier, plays are only for the rich. The only way any of the poor folk could see a play is to catch them when they're performed by churches. Our town is so small, we only got one church and they ain't got no time for plays."

"No, I get that. I mean, like, what happens in a play?"

Mr. Hemmindale stared at me. "You've really never heard of a play?"

I felt ashamed I'd been so poor that even the small amount of knowledge I did have was incomparable to what rich people knew. Having the learning Gift left me with the ability to read and write—but if there was nothing for me to read, I couldn't ever learn nothin' new. So, despite being fluent in many languages, I suddenly realized I was still very ... dumb ... in many different ways.

Mr. Hemmindale reached out a gloved hand and said, "You've gotta start somewhere if you wanna learn something, right? Don't worry, you're still young; you've got time." He straightened his coat with a smile, like he was proud to be able to teach me something. I smiled back. "A play is basically a form of entertainment, where folks pretend to be other folks for fun. They act out a story, basically."

"A story? So, it's like if the character from a book came to life?"

"Very good, Amana! That's exactly it!" He slapped his knee. "You're a very bright young girl, but all you seem to love is bein' a merchant. What a pity."

"Oh, Mr. Hemmindale, I love being a merchant, but I

love reading stories, too! Especially the adventurous stories from the Literature of the Scribes."

Mr. Hemmindale's smile began to fade, and I realized I'd spoken too much.

He couldn't look me in the eye as he said, "You can read much better than you've been pretending, can't you? Most stories aren't written in common language, they do that on purpose. The Scribes write everything in different languages so us common folk can't understand it. So," he took a breath, his eyes lifting to meet mine, "what have you been reading, Amana?"

I swallowed hard.

"Well, you've been lying, too." Mr. Hemmindale stepped back. "How dare you."

"You've been pretending to be a poor farmer! Ripping everyone off when you've got enough coin to run away and see fancy plays that are *only for rich folk*!" I pointed my finger, using his own words against him.

We stared at each other and finally Mr. Hemmindale said, "Amana, there's nothing wrong with being able to read. Even some women can read; but there's something else going on and you're trying to hide it from me."

I turned on my heels and ran out the barn to Ruby. As I climbed on, Ruby took off running, moving her short legs as hard as she could. I could hear Mr. Hemmindale hollering behind us, but I was too afraid to look back. Once we got close to my shack, I jumped off Ruby and ran to Ray's place.

"Ray!" I screamed. "Ray!"

"Amana? What's wrong?" Ray burst through the door, tearing the pelt hanging in the doorway aside. His eyes were wide open, and he was breathing hard.

Mrs. Castillo walked out behind him, swollen and pregnant. She looked just as worried as Ray as she said, "Amana, are you alright?"

"Ray," I whispered.

He hopped from the porch and ran right up to me. I grabbed his hand, but he pulled me into a hug instead. That made this so much harder. I wanted to cry into his dirty shirt as I mumbled against him, "Ray, I've gotta run tonight. I'm going to grab as many supplies as I can and I'm leaving tonight."

"Is something wrong?" Mrs. Castillo asked behind us.

Ray pulled away and yelled, "Just go back inside!"

In silence, she shuffled back into the small shack. Ray didn't speak again until he was sure she was gone. "Where is this coming from?" His eyes were on me, wide and full of emotions I couldn't name—fear? Anger? Sorrow?

I grabbed his hand and said, "Come with me."

We ran out to the well, hand in hand, no words spoken between us. Just the sound of the wind crying and the high grass whispering as it kissed our ashen knees. When we reached the brick well, we sat down and looked at each other. Ray was quiet but everything he wanted to say was written on his face. He didn't look shy or boyish anymore, this Ray before me, with lines in his face and words hidden in the corner of his frown, was a man.

I took a breath. "I saw Mr. Hemmindale today and he found out that I can read."

"That's not bad," he shrugged. "Women can read, too."

"But most women don't read books written in an uncommon language."

"How would he know what kind of books you read?" His frown deepened.

"I mentioned the Literature of Scribes. Almost all the books there are written in uncommon language. But I told him I enjoyed some of the work there." I stood and covered my face.

"That's not so bad."

"Ray, where would I have learned to read other languages? The only answer is that I have the Gift." I let out a hiccup, trying hard not to cry. "I have to get out of here before word spreads and they come for me."

Ray stood and pulled my hands from my face so he could hold them. "Alright. We'll meet back here."

I shook my head. "You can't go."

"Amana," he whispered. The sound of his voice broke my heart, but I couldn't let him ruin his life for me.

"No, Ray."

He grabbed me by the shoulders. "You can't go alone. Are you crazy?"

"*Ray*," I wriggled from his grasp. "You can't go. If I go, they'll come for me. But if you go, they'll come for your family."

"And what makes you so sure they won't come for yours?"

"I don't have a family worth anything," I said quietly, staring at the dry grass. "Nobody's gonna come for them. They'll chase me, but I can get ahead of them and flee tonight."

"I can't let you do that. I can't..." Ray's voice cracked right with my heart.

He dropped to his knees and let out a sob. He knew I was right. I hugged him, letting myself enjoy the way he held me tight, his strong arms around my waist as my hands ran through his wavy hair. I gasped and took in the nutty scent of his body; I'd never been held so close before. There was something bitter in that embrace, something heavy that made me want to let go. I didn't like the way my heart raced, I didn't like the way Ray cried so uncontrollably, like I was his whole world. I wasn't. He had a family; he had a sister on the way. And he had some other girl he was always thinkin' about. But here we were, saying goodbye like lovers, covered in tears and slobber. I hated it all. I desperately wanted something different to happen, someone to say it would be alright. But I was running with nowhere to go. I felt empty yet so loved as Ray held me and cried.

"Ray," I choked through tears, "please, you have to let me go. I have to go."

"Please don't go," he whispered, and my entire body ached. I didn't want to go. I didn't want to run without Ray. But I had to leave him in order to save him.

"I'll come back for you, Ray. But you have to let me go now." I pulled from him, feeling his grip loosen as we peeled apart. I gave him one last look before I turned away; I didn't whisper goodbye; I didn't say *I'll miss you*. Ray knew that already. I just turned and left, running all the way back to my shack in silence.

* * *

"Seems like you've got yourself into a bit of a mess, Favian." The words were like venom from the fangs of a snake. I was leaning against my front door, panting from the run, when I glanced up to see my mother standing before me.

"I don't have time for this." I tried to walk by so I could go pack my things, but she grabbed me by the collar and dragged me back.

I lost my footing, which she took advantage of by slamming me against the shack door. "I see you're writing now, Favian. What's this I'm hearing around town about a letter? You thought I wouldn't find out?" She pouted her lips at me, and suddenly I found myself staring not at my mother, but at a deranged woman.

"I knew you would find out," I said. "I just hoped I'd be long gone before that."

She shoved me to the ground, and I hit my face right on the floor. The pain burned through my entire head, but I didn't want to fight. I was running out of time. "Mother, please! I have to go," I cried.

"Go where? To scribal school? They..." A punch landed hard on face. "Will..." Another punch. "*NEVER!*" This time the punch hit my ribs, and she snatched my head up by my hair and whispered beside me, "accept you."

I was on the floor in the living room; the shack was still messy from our last brawl—knocked over furniture, pieces of the rocking chair lying about. This fight was not going to end like the last one. I grabbed a piece of Ma's broken rocking chair and slung it over my shoulder. A horrible cry flew from her lips and she let me go, falling to the floor and holding her face.

I wasted no time, scrambling away and running through the shack to gather supplies. I didn't need much, just enough for a day of travel. I had fruit, jam, and bread, a pouch of water, my coin purse, papers, ink, and the play I'd stolen from the scribal house. I wrapped everything into a cloth and then wrapped that over my head so I could walk with my hands free. It was an old-fashioned way of travelling, with all my goods balanced on my head, but I didn't mind. It reminded me of some of the old paintings I'd seen of my great-grandparents and their parents, too.

As I left my bedroom, I saw Ma sitting against the door. Her head was bleeding, but she didn't try to tend the wound; just sat staring at nothing until she lifted her head and said to me, "You finally fought back." Her voice was soft again, just like it used to be before she'd cracked from exhaustion. Mother was always so kind, but she'd also have days like today where her kindness wore thin, or her emotions fluctuated.

"Mother, I have to go. So please move," I said plainly.

"I know." She laughed lightly. "I tried so hard to keep you here, but you fought so hard to get away. Now look, you really will have to leave." Mother looked up at me and her face was saddened. "Do you know why I named you Favian? It wasn't my idea—I never would have given you a boy's name. It was God's idea. He named you."

I squinted. I'd never heard this story before. "What?"

"God named you. He said it would help you become someone He needed you to be one day. I remember when He told me; I was six months pregnant, and He spoke and said He'd anointed you to become a Scribe. But I had my doubts." Tears streamed from her eyes. "I gave you to God, and He said He would use you to do great things for Him as a Scribe. But I was afraid. We'd had trouble conceiving; you were our miracle child. I couldn't give you to this world and possibly never get you back!" She paused, and I could see her searching for words. "But God warned me the cost of rebellion. Now your father is sick, and I *have* to let you go for the both of us." She shook her head quietly. "Your father is the one paying the heaviest price for our rebellion. God is not to blame. He warned us, as all fathers do. Your father had dreams that he would fall ill, but he wouldn't budge, and neither would I. Instead, you budged and took heed to Him. Now I will lose you but gain your father back."

"You don't get to cry," I said finally.

"I know." Mother wiped her tears. "It ate at me every day!" She was yelling now. "It made me go insane, knowing I may lose you both. But I couldn't let you go. And today you showed me, I could never hold you back. Nor can I keep God's plans from happening. Please, Amana," she said sweetly, "forgive me and your father."

I stared down at the crying woman. She moved slowly from the front door and laid on the floor, sobbing. I knelt in front of her and sighed. "I forgive you." Then I stood and opened the door, the chilly night air engulfed my rage and cooled me quickly. "Take care of Ruby. Tell my father I forgive him. Goodbye, Mama."

I stepped forward and closed the door behind me.

Chapter Five
Favian Amana Hart

I walked forever, deep into the night, thinking about everything I was leaving behind. The market, the life of a merchant, friends, parents, Ruby, Ray, my entire town. It was a small place, insignificant compared to Sesame, where Ben lived. But it was mine and it was all I'd ever known.

I'd found it hard to leave Ray, but it was easy to leave my parents behind. After hearing what Ma had said, how we had to work so hard because of them, I was angry, and I was hurt. How could they do that to us? How could one knowingly walk into God's judgement? I didn't understand it. But I had to forgive them. I didn't want to think of Ray or even Ruby, though I did wonder if Ruby would miss me. It was weird, thinking about all these little things. I never realized how much Ruby meant to me, or the market, or even the way the fresh peaches from Mr. Hemmindale's farm smelled. I wondered if I would get to smell them again. But when I thought about all the fruit I liked, I remembered Mr. Hemmindale and how he'd been pretending to be a farmer, when he was really rich. *But why?* I wondered. Why would he live as a farmer when he had all that money? I wouldn't have gone back into that town to get his coin money if he hadn't fed me that story about falling behind without it.

The questions plagued my mind until I found a spot to lay down. I knew the nights would be cold, so I curled up into a tight ball and faced west, hoping to get the least amount of wind on my face. I drifted into a cold and shivering slumber, giving my brain a moment to stop wondering and upsetting myself.

When I woke, the sun was not up yet. It was still cool, and my body wouldn't stop shaking, but I knew I had to keep going. I thought hard about why I was running, how being a woman who could read beyond the normal comprehension was only known to be witchcraft. It amazed me how foolish people could be. Scribes have been around as long as time itself; how is it that all this time only men could become Scribes and not women? Not a single one.

That didn't make sense to me. I am a woman and I

know that I was born with the Gift. I know I'm meant to be a Scribe. And I know I can't be the first in history. I wanted to be angry, but my shivering body kept my temper leveled.

As I walked, I ate green grapes and sipped water from my satchel. The cold water made my shivering worse, so I didn't drink much. By the time I'd finished my vine of grapes, I'd entered a small town. It was a simple place, the kind of town you had to pass through to get to somewhere better.

I'd been through here many times on my deliveries. As I walked through the glum town, I noticed a small crowd gathered with someone speaking at the center.

I recognized the man's voice when he said, "I am looking for a little, brown peasant girl. She's wanted at the scribal house."

One woman fell at his feet and begged him, "It's me! Please take me!"

"Remove yourself from my sight, peasant!" he shouted, pushing her away.

The crowd grew; men and women pressed toward him, hoping he'd take them with him. I made my way through the crowd and brought myself right before Ben Jones. The tall man stared down at me before he sighed and said, "Come with me."

"I'm not going unless you tell me right here and now

what you want with me."

"Yeah!" a man cried.

Another hollered, "Whatever she can do, surely I can do better!"

The crowd began to buzz, but I ignored them, keeping my eyes on Ben who'd started to look worried. The increasingly angry mob grew louder until Ben finally caved in. "Alright, if you must know, the head of the scribal house has concerns about a letter you delivered on behalf of Favian Hart." A hush swept the crowd, and I could tell their focus shifted from Ben to me.

"And if I go with you, you swear before all these people that you won't hurt me or my loved ones?"

"I'm not sure what a band of poor misfits could do but—"

"It doesn't matter, just say you swear." I never looked away from Ben. His apple red face burned with nerves.

He said, "I swear we will not hurt you in any capacity nor your family."

"Good."

"Let's go now. I will be shamed no further with this group of low lives."

"Hey! You better watch your mouth!" A fat finger pointed in Ben's face, but he swatted it away and turned to leave.

"I've got a horse just up there," he said to me.

Ben and I did not speak for the entire ride. I had a bit of adjusting to do on the horse, but once I got used to the feeling, Ben sped up and we rode swiftly back to the scribal house. When we arrived, the older man I'd met the first time was waiting outside. He was holding the letter I'd left him.

"I hear you stole quite a deal of money from us." I didn't answer. "I got the letter you left. The one about the great warrior. How did he find out about the missing pages?" I only blinked. Annoyed, the pale man tried to contain his temper as he said, "This Favian man, why did he send you? Do you know him?"

"Her."

Now it was his turn to stand there blinking. "I—I beg your pardon?" he stuttered.

"Do I know *her*? Yes," I explained.

The man looked at Ben and then back at me. "What are you saying? That Favian is a woman?"

"Yes."

"Blasphemy!"

Before I knew it, I was hurled over, holding a stinging cheek. I'd been slapped.

Panting the man said, "Do you know I could kill you where you stand? Spreading lies like that is very dangerous! There is no way Favian could be a woman! The language used is far beyond what we have allowed women to learn in our society. So, I'll ask you again; who is Favian?"

I straightened myself up and looked him in the eye. "I am."

Just as he was about to hit me again, I said, "In the beginning was the Word, and the Word was with God, and the Word was God. He was in the beginning with God. John chapter one verses one and two."

Ben's eyes nearly fell from his sockets, while the older man stood frozen.

"That's what I wrote in Arabic at the end of the letter. Women are only allowed to read the Old Testament. All of the New Testament is written in a language we are not allowed to learn. In my town, the New Testament is written in Arabic. You can check if you'd like. That's why Ben has been traveling around to find Favian, by seeing which town's Literature of Scribes holds a New Testament Bible written in Arabic. It's my town, Blakenberge. I am Favian Amana Hart."

"She has to be him, my lord." Ben had found his voice instead of staring at us with his mouth open and his eyes all bugged out. "She was here the day those papers were delivered with that story. She must've heard you talking about it."

The old man looked dizzy. He grabbed his head and sat on the stairs of the front porch.

"I published that letter in your town's newspaper," I

said. "Word has already reached Blakenberge. But the people of my town are foolish and can't read very well. Which means, for now, your secret is safe. But people will eventually wonder if Favian is from that town, and when they find the New Testament written in Arabic, they'll know for certain."

"You're lying! You copied the words!" the old man said.

"How could I translate words I couldn't understand? How could I tell you the story 'Achilles' if I couldn't read uncommon language, or formal language? How could I tell you what was in a letter if I couldn't read it and only delivered it? How could I tell you what was in a letter I didn't write?"

The pale man blinked rapidly as he uttered, "This cannot be." His chin wobbled as he shook his head in disbelief. "This cannot be."

"I am a Scribe," I said plainly. "And you can't tell me otherwise."

"There is no way!" the man yelled. He was sweating and breathing hard.

I balled my hands into fists. "All those girls you turned away from the school, all those women you sentenced to death for witchcraft, it all weighs on your shoulders. I am proof you were wrong to hurt them. I am proof your organization is full of liars. I am a woman, and I am a Scribe, and there's no way you can deny me. Not with my name floating around now. You've been waiting on Favian ... here I am."

"I will not teach you." The man stood to leave, but I called out, "You don't have to. I can read and teach myself. Just give me a place to stay."

"I will not!"

"Then I will tell everyone."

"And who will believe you?" He stamped his foot, but it was a childish, petty action.

I raised an eyebrow. "Everyone will believe me when I read from the Bible—when I prove that I can understand the New Testament, especially all the parts that tell us women *can* be leaders."

"How dare you threaten me!"

I stepped closer to him, right in his sweaty face. "I'm not afraid anymore. If I die, I die. But my name cannot be killed, and for God's honor, I will not die in vain."

"What if we kept you here as a Scribe?" Ben suggested, earning stares from the pale man and myself. I honestly didn't know how to reply—I'd expected a bigger fight from him, considering how rude he'd been since I'd met him. *And* the fact that he'd **tried to kill me** before.

He ignored our stares and said, "What if we let you stay, but you were not allowed to leave without our permission, and we put all your writing in your name but left Favian as a mystery?"

"Ben, do you hear yourself?" the old man wheezed. "I am the Scribe and the head of the scribal house; I make the decisions!"

He glanced over at him, his eyes cutting him down in one judgmental tick. *That* was the Ben I knew. "You're making a bad decision, my lord. I'm supposed to help when I think your choices are being swayed."

The old man moved his mouth, but Ben cut him off. "Listen, Mr. Marlowe, I can't keep pretending anymore. Scribes aren't born every day; we've been waiting for the next one since I was a child. I don't want this filthy peasant here either, but if our institution can claim we have the next Scribe, then we can finally move forward. No one ever has to know it's her."

Mr. Marlowe stood there staring at me, thinking hard, like he knew Ben was right. "You will attend to her," he finally said. "But she and I will have no dealings—*none at all*, Ben!" With that, he turned and ran into the house, leaving Ben and I outside.

We stood there for a moment until Ben turned to me. "I didn't do this for you."

"I didn't say thank you."

"Well, that's rather rude to say to the one man who just gave you a spot as a Scribe."

"No," I crossed my arms. "You gave *Favian* a spot as a Scribe, not me."

Chapter Six
The Act

As the months passed, I thought less and less of my life before becoming a Scribe. Dwelling on the past and everything I'd left behind was just a burden. I couldn't focus on my studies carrying around all those extra thoughts. As time went on, they tormented me less and my daily training filled the void.

For the first three months of training, I practiced formal writing in various languages while reading books at different comprehension levels. With each book I read, I had to do a thorough analysis on the story and provide a translation for one chapter of each book, in the language assigned to me.

Those months were torture. I was just a little goldfish,

a *pet fish*, thrown into a vast ocean, where the fish there were not small. Everyone around me knew so much more than me; being a fast learner did not compensate for how much I had to cram into my head. Not only did I have to read and understand everything I read, but I also had to learn things like grammar, punctuation, metaphors, and plots. There was so much to learn within the literary world that almost made the Gift alone seem like child's play.

Eventually, things smoothed out. Either I got smarter, or I got used to the mental torture. With the bit of knowledge I'd learned, I had to apply that to some stories I'd been given. It was just a few that were missing sentences and punctuation—small fixes that wouldn't change the entire story, but rather elevate it. I liked this work; it was exciting to fill in the missing pages with my own ideas. Ben told me these sorts of tasks would help me become more creative. Everything I did was checked by Ben before it could be sent off for publishing. He approved most of it, but sometimes he'd make me rework the same sentence 50 times before it fit perfectly in the puzzle of the story.

"Amana, read that again and tell me if it makes sense," he snapped in that snooty voice of his.

I took the pages back and read quietly. It was a simple story, but Ben wanted there to be elements of illusion present.

"I guess it *doesn't?*"

He raised a single, dark eyebrow. "Are you asking me?"

"*No?*" I asked anyway. Ben rolled his eyes.

Ben and I had grown close over the months, as odd as that may seem. We worked hard every day, and when I had time off, I spent it visiting the theatres with him. He was still a snob, but he valued the Gift more than anything, and he wanted only to serve the scribal house, not to oppose it. So, I guess Ben didn't really like me, he just respected me because I had the Gift, but that didn't matter to me. He was nicer than before, and he'd stopped calling me a peasant. So that was something.

"Amana," he said, interrupting my thoughts, "you know the importance of creativity. We have to create history, and a world people want to live in through literature."

"I know, Ben. I just have a hard time lying about history, although it's not like anyone would know the truth. I still feel bad for changing these stories."

"You have a hard time changing stories and making them better for the benefit of the people, but you seem to find it awfully easy to steal."

I looked up from the papers, but Ben was focused on his own work. I sighed and flopped down in the chair across from him. "I was going to give them back."

"After you made edits and filled in the plays the way you wanted?"

"Wait, how'd you know about the other one?"

He finally looked up at me, tired eyes filled with annoyance. "Because I am an assistant to you and Mr. Marlowe, which means I have access to all your writings and right now he's missing two works."

"I just wanted to practice writing since I can't write anything myself right now. I thought being a Scribe was about writing, not fixing all these old books."

"Amana, you're not ready to write your own works yet. Until you are, you need to continue to work on the assignments I have given you."

"How am I not ready? It's been over eight months now and I still can't write my own work? You took all the edits and backstory I made to the Iliad, and you even kept the character name. How can you say I'm not ready when you used my work before? I thought you said I was good." I sank deeper into my chair and folded my arms like a child.

Ben sighed. "Favian, you are good. But you're also a rare case. We have never had a woman as a Scribe, and you weren't privy to any knowledge before this. The little you learned before becoming a Scribe doesn't even amount to what we test our young boys on when checking for the Gift. Yes, what you came up with for the Iliad was absolutely astonishing from the small bit of knowledge you had, but at this level, to produce your own work, you've got to top the Iliad and Marlowe doesn't think you can.

You have progressed, but not enough. There's still very much for you to learn and understand about the scribal world."

"Then teach me!" I stood up, my chair scraped against the floor with the movement, screaming out exactly the way I wanted to.

Ben's eyes lazily dragged from my angry face down to the screeching chair, his eyebrow pointed at the ceiling again. "You're not ready."

"I *am* ready!" I slammed my hands on his desk.

"Favian Amana Hart, you are not ready and that is *final*."

Tears swelled in my eyes as I realized that not even Favian could make it in. I looked at the pages beneath my fists; the written words blurred through my tears. I said, "How could I be ready if I'm never taught how to compose a play, a story, a novel? How could I not be ready when I produced good enough work for the Iliad with no training? I have training now, so how much better am I? But I see now." I sniffled. "I'm stuck here, only to do the work Christopher Marlowe is too busy for. It isn't even about my skill level, is it? You're afraid to take a chance that someone might know Favian is a girl."

Ben was silent, staring straight ahead like he didn't even see me—like he didn't *want* to see me.

"I'm right, aren't I?" I yelled. I shook my head and tears streamed down my face. "This was just a setup to get me off the streets and under Christopher's thumb. Keep me quiet. I was so naïve. I was never going to get a real chance, and I was foolish to believe I ever would." I picked up my papers from his desk. "I will work on this to try to get it right by evening." Then I turned to leave.

Ben was still sitting there, his mouth closed tightly. He wasn't angry, but he looked defeated.

* * *

By evening, I'd given Ben a sentence he approved of, and I'd given one of the works I'd stolen from Mr. Marlowe a heavy dosage of ink. If I could not be Favian Amana Hart, then by all means, I would be someone else if it meant I could produce my own work.

* * *

I was angry, I was hurt, I was bitter. I prayed all night, begging God for freedom from these shackles. I'd walked right into a trap, but I had to believe there was good to come of this. I wanted to pack my things and leave through the night, but I couldn't run again. I'd come too far to give up. I *had* to succeed, there were countless women waiting on someone to help them, and God chose me. *How could I walk away now?*

I reasoned with myself day in and day out. I tossed and turned at night, desiring nothing more than to get a wink of sleep. But I couldn't. I had to work, I had to do something, I had to become something. But what? How could Favian Amana Hart become a Scribe without Ben and Christopher Marlowe stopping me? How could I change history?

Maybe I need to start smaller, I thought to myself late one night in bed.

"I should start small, just releasing some of my own stories. But they've gotta be great." I rolled onto my belly. "And they've gotta take attention away from Christopher Marlowe..." I paused, staring at the blank wall, then gasped as an idea hit me. "That's it! I have to be *better* than Marlowe. But not as Favian. If I do it as Favian, Marlowe might reveal that I'm a woman and say I'm working witchcraft. But, if I pretend to be someone else and gain some popularity, the crowds will be focused on the *fake* me. While readers are distracted with a pretend author, the *real* Favian can release small works. Not enough to cause a commotion, but enough to give myself a little bit of my own standing ground." I smiled, thinking that my plan was excellent. Then, as natural as anything I've ever done, I whispered, "I've gotta tell Ray!" Then all the sadness came rushing back. I wiped my smile away as I covered my mouth, like I'd said something I shouldn't have.

"Ray," I whispered.

His name was sweet on my lips, summoning a sudden rush of emotion I thought I'd locked away for good. I curled into a ball, lying on my bunched up covers as tears spilled from my eyes. I missed him so much. But I'd been consumed by my training, by my writing, by stupid Ben Jones that I'd almost forgotten Ray. I didn't want to forget him, and I desperately wanted to see him again. In my desperation, I moved to my desk and began to write.

Dear Ray,

I hope this letter finds you well. It's been a very long time since I've seen you. How are you? How is your family? How are my parents? I hate to ask, but I often wonder if you still think of us as friends. I always believed we would be friends and merchants together forever. Now, "forever" seems like such a distant dream, I've nearly forgotten who I used to be.

I miss you Ray, and if it weren't for my will to stay, I would think of you often and find my way back to you.

I realized in this distance that I have found myself smiling the most when I write something good, and when I think of you. After eight long months of extensive training, I have found that my passion for the work of a Scribe is not fading, instead it is growing. But I noticed, recently, that my desire to see you again is not fading, either; it's growing more rapidly than my passion for writing. However, I know I must put away these feelings as I'm sure you've forgotten me, and there's no way I could see you again. Well, at least not now.

I hate to tell you, but I'm stuck, Ray. I made it to the scribal school, but it is not as glamorous as I'd hoped. I'm in a situation I have no way out of without God and a dash of creativity. Right now, I am no more than a secretary. I am not what you would call an actual Scribe; I merely fill in the blanks Christopher Marlowe overlooked. I thought I loved it until I found out that I could never publish any work of my own. They have me here to keep Favian under their control, and I fell right into their hands. I thought I was smart enough, but I have come to learn just how smart everyone else is. But being smart isn't a criterion for God, just a willing and open heart. And I have that, and I will have God's name glorified no matter the cost, even if that cost is my name.

Sometime soon, Ray, I want to see you again, and I hope you'll want to see me. I'll be on my way to you when you hear of my new name, William Shakespeare.

When I finished writing, I folded the letter and sealed it in an envelope with the wax stamp Ben had custom made for me. It was a pure silver stamp with a cherry wood handle. The engraving in the silver was a heart with the letter "A" in the middle. I'd never used my wax stamp, as I'd never written anything worth sealing.

After I sealed Ray's letter, I sealed my finished copy of 'Henry VI' into a large envelope like the ones I'd seen Ben use to send off special works from Marlowe. Although my seal did not match the names I'd scribbled onto the envelope, I wanted my seal to begin to surface because, one day, it would belong to me again.

I left early the next morning to deliver the envelopes to the mailing center. I was not allowed to leave the house but neither Ben nor Marlowe woke up at normal times. They always worked late into the night and slept heavily into the day. By the time I'd returned, neither of them had awakened. But I gave myself no time to spare. As soon as I got home, I began working on the other play about shrewish women. I'd taken it from Mr. Marlowe weeks ago when he and Ben went out to watch Mr. Marlowe's play, "The Jew of Malta." Its release had taken the nearby towns by storm; everyone wanted to perform it.

I changed the name of the second play I stole from *Leashing my Shrewish Wife* to something I felt was a bit less derogatory, *The Taming of the Shrew*. This piece was particularly easy to work with for me. I changed a lot of details in the story while keeping the plot. Mr. Marlowe's version wasn't very good. Instead of a play about oppressing women, I wanted it to take a look at gender roles and realize how absurd they can be sometimes. But I feared the influential rich heads wouldn't like it if I was too bold, so I played with the theme. I kept gender roles intact, but I styled this particular play to ask the question, *Do gender roles really exist, or is this an aspect of our culture we've created on our own?*

I wanted to get the minds of the audience thinking of women having a different role in society without making it so obvious. If William Shakespeare is going to be a man of great stature, it wouldn't be wise to disagree with the common mindset. I had to remember my place in society as Shakespeare while always embedding another meaning into my plays. I wanted there to be things left up to the reader's interpretation, in the hopes that women would interpret it as a self-help guide.

While ladies were reading and watching the plays, so were gentlemen, and *The Taming of the Shrew* would be particularly eye catching for them. I knew they wouldn't enjoy such a dominating woman, so I made up a character, Katherina, to be more submissive to her husband. I gave her character more importance, but let the other woman go unpunished for her disobedience to her husband.

Despite this drama, I was certain Katherina's submission would be more satisfying than any disobedient wife.

The changes I made to the story almost made it unrecognizable as Mr. Marlowe's work. That was the goal. While I desired recognition of my talents, I also hoped the alterations in these plays, *Henry VI* and *The Taming of the Shrew*, would show Mr. Marlowe and Ben Jones what it felt like to be wiped from history.

Chapter Seven
Good News and Old Feelings

Three weeks passed and I went to the mailing center to send off *The Taming of the Shrew*. When I arrived, there were three letters waiting for me; one from the church I'd sent my play to, the second from a different church further east in the Mountains of Korse, and the last letter was from Ray. All three were addressed to, "The Assistant of William Shakespeare." I only left the postal code for return, but no delivery address, that way it would stay at the mailing center.

I rushed home to open the letters. When I returned, Ben and Marlowe were still asleep and had no idea I'd left, so I tiptoed up to my room and closed the door with a hush. I sat on my creaky bed and curled up tight to read.

All three letters sat there on display; all three were for me. My own mail. I couldn't stop myself from smiling. I decided to save Ray's letter for last, reading in the order I'd received them. The first was the reply from St. Matthew's Church. They adored *Henry VI* and wanted permission to perform the play. They also mentioned they passed the script to another church they thought would be interested and requested a second copy. If I permit them to perform, they'd pay me for copies of the script for their actors as well as a percentage of the proceeds from the performances.

I covered my mouth as my eyes darted over the letter, soaking up the black ink as fast as possible. Excitement oozed from me as I moved to the second letter. It came from a Lutheran church even further east than St. Matthew's. They said they also loved the work and would love to perform the piece if possible. They also promised payment for script copies as well as from performance proceeds. While I wasn't sure of the size of the Lutheran church of the mountains, I had to assume it was pretty big to be in direct connection with St. Matthew's—which was utterly huge. I'd heard about St. Matthew's from Ben; he often sent plays there on behalf of Mr. Marlowe. I figured a rising dramatist could use the exposure they'd be able to provide.

While the other two letters were exciting, I wasn't sure

what Ray would say to me. Though I'd hoped he would reply, I wasn't confident that he would. As I opened the letter, there was a wave of nostalgia that hit me. I could smell Ray on the paper; his husky scent, so strong and pungent. I tore open the envelope.

Amana?

Is this really you? I can't believe you are alive. I only knew for certain it was you because I remembered your handwriting—it was always so wispy. I'm glad to hear from you, I've been mourning you all this time. I've cried countless nights, and I have lost myself in the thought of your death. Why have you never written until now? For nearly nine months, I've longed for any news from you, but nothing ever came. I've been doing more runs for Mr. Hemmindale, and in every town, I read newspapers to find your name, but it was never there. I've truly missed you Amana, more than my poor heart can bear.

I wish you'd reached out earlier; I would've come to rescue you. I would give anything to see you again; to hug you, smell you, even see your curly hair. Why, Amana? Why did you never write? I'm so angry, but I am so relieved you're alive. You were the anchor that kept me from drifting away, and even when I thought you died, your memories anchored me still. I held onto you, even if I knew you weren't ever coming back. I wanted to make something of myself—become a man I hoped you'd be proud of.

You say you'd nearly forgotten yourself, but I believe I have totally forgotten myself. I became so obsessed with giving your life meaning that I stopped living the life I loved. But I feel alive again, knowing you are somewhere close by; only a day's journey away, and you could be in my arms.

I will wait for you Amana, because my feelings will never change. I have always loved you, and I will never stop. So please come back to me quickly. Write to me again soon and this time, tell me you love me.

"Ray loves me?" I asked aloud. I could feel my heart starting to race. As I tried to calm down, a feeling of excitement and embarrassment rolled over me. And then someone knocked on my door.

"One moment!" I shouted, shoving the three letters under my blankets. Whoever it was knocked again, and I nearly fell off my bed, diving for my robes as I said, "Come in!"

Ben opened the door just as I yanked my headwrap off. I only wear it when I go out, he would've been suspicious if he'd seen me in it. I'd gotten it off in time, but my hair was wild underneath. I looked like what my mother would call, a hot mess.

Ben blinked at me.

"Um, I was just getting decent," I explained.

He smirked, but that was all the reaction I got out of him. Then I realized how stupid I was acting. Ben only had eyes for books. I guess if I was a story, he'd like me somewhat. But right now, I was just silly Amana, covering up for no reason.

He leaned against the doorway, as pristine and fresh as he always looked in his pressed clothes and golden pocket watch winking as the sun from my window hit it at just the right angle. "I am running to the mailing center, and to the market. If you need something while I'm gone—"

"I know, I have to do it myself. I got it." I turned away

and started wrapping my hair up, just to cover the mess.

Ben sighed over my shoulder. "How long are you going to be childish and quiet like this?"

I chuckled and turned to face him. That's when I saw through his clean clothes and shiny jewelry. Ben had dark circles beneath his eyes, lines in his middle-aged face, and his exhausted expression seemed intense.

I smiled and said, "Not for much longer."

Ben squinted, sweeping his eyes around the room. He knew something was wrong, but he couldn't figure out what. Without another word, he turned and pulled the door shut behind him.

***

Two weeks after I received the letters from the churches, Ben told me he'd be taking a trip to St. Matthew's with Mr. Marlowe. They were going to discuss urgent matters with a play. I nodded, but I felt uneasy.

"We'll be gone for one week exactly. I have left food and work for you to finish until we return. There is more than enough to keep you busy well into the night, so you will have no reason to leave this house. Understood?" Ben looked down at me, and I felt an old rage stir.

"Understood," I said darkly.

Without a second thought, Ben placed his hat on his

head and left. It was quiet in the house. I'd never been left alone, but this matter was urgent enough for Ben *and* Marlowe to leave me. They'd received word this afternoon from St. Matthew's and left as quickly as they could. Marlowe seemed upset, even Ben seemed rattled. I was nervous about what St. Matthew's could possibly want, but with this opportunity of quiet, I decided to skip out on the work Ben left me, and instead continued working on script copies for the churches.

"I wish I had an assistant or someone to help me write these out," I murmured, flexing my numb fingers. I was hunched at my desk, the fading sunlight pouring in, making my papers glow. The worst part of being a writer was dealing with ink stains. The tips of my fingers were always black from smudging the ink and dipping my quill. I stared at the dark blotches on my hands, it looked so odd against my dark brown skin—even weirder when I saw it stained on Ben's fingers. He was pale and fair, and the black ink almost made him glow. I laughed out loud, then realized how ghostly it sounded here all alone.

I sang hymns while I wrote, hoping the time would pass sooner. My voice echoed through the empty schoolhouse, loud and soft at the same time. As I worked, I started humming a hymn Ray always loved to hear me sing; it wasn't long before I was smiling, thinking of him and his letter. I stared at the script I'd been copying; *maybe I should write to Ray again. With Marlowe and Ben gone, I won't have to sneak out to the mailing center.* As I reached for my letter paper, I said, "Wait, I can go *see* Ray!"

I scrambled to clean up my writing supplies and ran through the house to pack. My town was only a day's journey. I was going home. I was going to see Ray. Except he wasn't the only person in town I'd left behind. There were other things at home I wasn't ready to face. Suddenly, I slowed my pace, a change of clothes still in my hand as I clutched a cloth sack, standing in the middle of my room.

"What if someone recognizes me? What if Ray *doesn't* recognize me? What about my parents? How will I face them again?" I sighed and sat on my bed. I knew I'd changed mentally, but it wasn't until that moment that I realized my body had changed, too.

I was always a small girl, but I'd grown quite a bit, and only in the way it would matter to my husband—if I had one. I'd truly begun to fit the image of a woman. When I thought of that, I feared that Ray's confession would be nothing more than ink pressed to paper. But why did it mean so much that Ray confessed? I didn't want to focus on those embarrassing thoughts anymore, so I gathered myself and finished packing for the trip.

"I'll leave tonight," I said as I looked in the mirror. "That way it'll be early morning when I arrive, and I can meet Ray at the market."

I picked through my clothes; I only wore a few different outfits by choice. While Ben and Marlowe kept me prisoner here, Ben at least treated me properly. My wicker bin was full of garments, some even worth gold callios. I wanted to look nice to Ray, but what if he didn't like the way the rich clothes looked on me? I longed for the rags I'd arrived with, but Ben had gotten rid of those the moment I'd entered the house. He placed me in a bath, and while I washed, he fetched me a completely new wardrobe. I pulled out a few pieces now that I thought might impress Ray, and face-paint Ben had purchased for me. He told me I would need it when people began requesting my appearance at their functions but, little did I know, Ben was just playing the part.

When I finally gathered everything, I took one more item from Marlowe; a suit. It was one I'd never seen him wear. As I left his room, I saw a satchel sitting on the floor. Marlowe was never one to carry a bag, and my curiosity ate away at me as I stared at it. I reached in and felt a cool piece of metal, a handgun. I pulled my hand out of the bag quickly and stared at the satchel. For whatever reason, I decided to take that, too.

After travelling all night, I arrived at the market in my hometown. It was early morning so there were only a few people there. I tied my horse to the tree and watched the merchants from afar. I scanned the few people and noticed a familiar figure working hard to set up a tent. It was Mr. Castillo. I watched the man in his straw hat hammer away at a tent peg, while Mrs. Castillo brought him more pegs, walking slowly with a baby tied to her back. A small smile stretched across my face, and tears began to swell. As I looked around the market, vivid memories of my early mornings replayed in my mind.

I watched in silence, turning my gaze to two men and a woman nearing the Castillo's tent. Their faces seemed to blur for a moment, and then I recognized the woman as Ma. She looked radiant—completely different from the deranged state she'd been in when I'd left. Her face was glowing; she looked well-rested, not exhausted and overworked like she'd always been before. When I looked from Ma to the two men, I recognized my father first. He was awake and walking. But he had a bad limp, and the man who helped him walk was Ray.

I held my chest and gasped for air. I'd longed to see Ray, and I finally had. I don't know if it was the distance, or the time we'd been apart, but, in that moment, I finally saw in Ray the thing that made every woman swoon over him.

Without thinking, I stepped forward. In my ground sweeping dress, I approached my family from the market outskirts. They were talking and laughing like a real family. Like a happy family. They all looked so joyous without me.

Smiles I'd never seen before plastered their faces, like radiant beams of sunshine. Was I the reason no one had ever smiled before?

I stopped walking and stood in the thick grass. I watched Ray help my father sit, and my mother unload a cart attached to Ruby. Even Ruby made happier grunts. It felt like I'd been run over by a horde of horses. I was suddenly winded, and my face felt fuzzy. My nose burned and my eyes could not hold the swelling tears. Why were they so happy without me? I thought Ray loved me. Why did my family replace me? I always thought I'd see everyone smile when we made it out of Blakenberge, but I was wrong. They'd started smiling when I'd left Blankenberge.

I wanted to call to them, but my voice fell silent. In a feeling of regret and defeat, I turned and started back. As I walked to my horse, I heard a rustling noise behind me. My heart leapt into my throat—someone had found me. Someone had come to take me back to the scribal house.

I ran the rest of the way to my horse and pulled out the small handgun from the satchel. Before I knew it, I had turned and aimed. Hands flew up, and I realized my gun was pointed right at his chest. I recognized the stitching in his shirt as my mother's, and when our eyes finally met, he said, "Amana?"

"Ray?" I whispered.

"Amana!" Ray exclaimed. He moved forward but I

cocked the gun, stopping him in his tracks.

"Whoa! Wait a second, what's going on? It's me, Ray," he spoke gently and that made me even angrier.

"I know who you are," I choked. Ray looked like a man. He was stronger than I'd ever seen him, and he was more handsome than before. His thin figure had changed into a working gentleman.

"Then lower the gun, Amana. What's wrong?"

"Cut the crap, Ray! I seen you down there with my parents. Everyone is happier without me. So don't try an' keep me here. I'm leavin', since all of you are *so* happy. What do you need rescuing for?"

"Amana, you've got it all wrong." He moved forward and I gripped the gun tighter.

"You take one more step and I will blow a hole right through you," I seethed with anger and disgust that I could become so jealous in the flicker of a moment. Why was it hurting so badly to see the people I loved …? My thoughts trailed off as I realized why it hurt so much. Because I loved them, all three of them. The thought of loving Ray made me feel sick with an ungodly anger.

I couldn't explain my emotions, but I was losing control when Ray said, "Amana, please, listen."

"I thought you loved me, Ray!" I yelled. The worried look on his face morphed into sadness. He didn't move or speak as I began to sob.

I clutched the gun in my shaking hands and said, "I thought you only loved me. But you've replaced me and made my family into a family again. Something I longed to do." I choked on a sob. "I was stupid enough to believe you loved me for me. But I found myself in a mess of chaos because the one person I wanted to rescue more than anyone else doesn't seem to need saving at all. Even after I've fallen in love with him."

Overwhelmed, my grip on the gun became weak, but Ray was there. He moved quickly, knocking the gun away so he could pull me into a tight hug. His dirty shirt smelled familiar, and his embrace felt like home.

"I have always loved you, Amana," he whispered, his voice muffled against the fabric of my headwrap. "I've been waiting all this time for you to come back home—to come back to me. You are the girl I've been waiting on."

After I'd wiped all my tears away, Ray asked me to wait for him in the flower field nearby. I lay in the grass, trying to beat back the thoughts of leaving that kept snaking into my head. I was nervous, but I knew I couldn't run. Not again. I was always running from problems or running into them, it seemed.

I don't know what I was thinking. That confession came out without any planning or hesitation. I told Ray that I'd fallen in love with him! Now, all I wanted to do was hide, but I couldn't deny the warmth that rolled over me whenever I thought of the smile he'd had on his face. Or the way he'd hugged me. I wanted to see Ray. I wanted to talk to him and laugh like the old times. I needed him. But as nervous and excited as I was, there was also a small sense of fear wrapped up in there. There wouldn't be much time for laughing. There was only five days left until Ben Jones and Mr. Marlowe came back. Then I wouldn't be able to see Ray again for a while. I didn't want to leave again, but I knew what God had called me to do, and I couldn't do it in Blakenberge.

While I waited, I took some paper I'd packed and wrote down an idea. *When I confessed to Ray that I loved him, I held a gun in my hand, but I didn't want to kill him. How could I live without him?* That thought bounced through my head, entangled with the words from Ray's letter about me being his anchor. *What would Ray have done if it'd been confirmed that I'd died? What would I have done if I accidentally shot Ray? I couldn't live with myself.* I stared at the paper and, with my thoughts swirling, I began another play. This one would be about the tragic romance of young love.

Deep into the evening I wrote out scenes for a play. I came up with character names, and stage settings that would bring out the message even stronger. I'd only taken a few breaks to finish one copy of scripts requested from the churches. The overwhelming story of my new play captivated me so deeply I didn't hear Ray walk up.

"Amana? What are you doin'?"

"Ray!" I squealed. "You scared me!" I shot to my feet and dusted the dirt from my dress. When I looked at Ray, his eyes softened. They looked mystified, as if he were looking at someone he *almost* recognized.

"Amana, you've changed." The words hit me like daggers.

"Did I? I really can't tell." I flailed my fancy dress around in embarrassment, desperately wishing for the dirty rags Ben had thrown away.

"I mean..." Ray moved forward confidently. He stepped close to me and placed his hand on the small of my back. A chill made me shudder and stand perfectly straight as Ray's other hand swept over to gently move a loose curl from my face. I frowned at it, surprised I'd let one slip from my headscarf.

"You've aged gracefully," Ray murmured. His voice made me want to melt, and the look in his eyes made me wonder who taught the lanky boy from before to be so confident.

"I have to say," I placed my hand on his firm chest, "you've changed a lot, too."

He chuckled. "My father told me you only get one chance to capture the heart of the woman you love, and I thought I'd missed my chance when you left. But this time,

I won't let you get away."

So, it was Mr. Castillo who'd birthed this newfound confidence in Ray. His own father had given him advice, reinforced the love I hadn't known had been there all along. That mystery girl he'd told me about before I left ... could he have been talking about me all along?

Suddenly, my lips felt warm.

Ray's hands moved from my back to my face, and then to the scarf covering my hair. He'd always hated the scarves, hated that I had to hide my hair, and that showed as he tangled his hands into the fabric of my wrap and gave it a gentle tug. It came loose and fell onto my shoulders; I gasped as my thick braid rolled down my back.

"Why did you do that?" I snapped, pulling away.

Ray smiled, and it was as warm as I remembered. "Because a woman of your background cannot show her hair, except in front of her husband."

"Yeah, so?" I fumbled around, trying to untangle the scarf from my shoulders so I could wrap my hair again. I was angry and grumbling to myself. Ray was a man; he had no idea how annoying it was to wear these things. They were convenient when my hair was acting up, but when I was legally required to wear them, they were just a burden.

"Why do you even care if I have to hide my hair?" I grunted.

When Ray didn't answer, I glanced up from my scarf and nearly fainted. He was kneeling in the grass with a shining piece of metal held delicately between two fingers.

"Favian Amana Hart, will you become Favian Amana Castillo?" He swallowed nervously, allowing a shadow of the boy I remembered to flash across his face. "Will you marry me?"

I looked around the field of flowers and tried to catch my breath. I had rewritten work for literary masters, had trained at the scribal house for months, had developed my own plays and a completely new identity just to publish them. But now, with Ray on his knees and a ring in his hand, I was lost for words. With tears in my eyes, I extended a shaky hand to him and watched as he placed the little silver ring on my finger.

Finally, I managed to say, "Yes! I'll marry you."

Chapter Eight
Me and All of Who I Am

I finally decided on the title, "Romeo and Juliet," for my romantic tragedy. I wanted this play to tug on heart strings and encourage people to view romance in a different way. *Instead of forcing young women to marry, let them fall in love, as I did,* I thought while I wrote. I'd been staying at an inn a few miles out from the market. It was as run down as the Castillo's shack, but I didn't mind. It reminded me of my humble beginnings, and often those memories were some I enjoyed reflecting on the most.

As I wrote, I heard a knock at the door. I knew it was Ray—he visited me every night before he went home. I hadn't told him I had to return to the scribal house yet, but I decided I would tonight since I had only two days left.

Another knock sounded at the door, and I pranced over and opened it.

"Hey," Ray said. His smile was worn, and his face was tired.

"Was it rough today?" I stepped aside to let him in, leaning against the frame of the door as he moved through the small room.

"It was," he sighed, taking off his hat. "It was beyond tiring today. There was an awful lot of customers. More than a normal Tuesday would bring in." He flopped down on my bed, still going on about the market but I was already lost in my thoughts, wondering how I should tell him I'd be leaving soon. I could feel the muscles in my back tightening from my anxiety; dampness melted into my shirt as I began to sweat.

"You alright?"

"Hmm?"

I glanced up from the floor and found Ray squinting at me. "Oh!" I waved him off. "I'm fine."

"What's wrong?"

"Really, Ray, I'm fine."

Ray came over to me. "You can tell me anything," he said softly.

Those words were gate openers. I'd been quiet about what really had been going on at the scribal house, even though Ray had been asking. I told him I wanted to just talk about the old times and catch up with him. But I'd pushed this away for too long.

"Sit down, Ray." I grabbed his calloused hands and pulled him to the small table nearby. He was looking at me with an expression I couldn't name. Worry? Confusion? Sadness?

I took a breath. "Ray, I have to return home."

"Amana, you are home," he said.

"You know what I mean. I have to go back to the scribal house. If I don't return, Ben will come looking for me."

"He won't know where you're at, will he?"

"No, but I don't want him to come looking for me. Besides, I *am* still a Scribe."

"You're also a fiancé now. That means we have to start doing things together."

I sighed and reached for Ray's hand. "I'll be back, I promi—"

"When?" he snapped. "Because I didn't even know you were alive a few days ago."

"I don't know when. I have to wait for another opening."

"Another *opening*." He said the words like they were poisonous. I nearly winced. "Who knows when that'll be? You said it yourself, they have you in the house to keep you under their thumb. They have nothing for you there, so why go back? You have the opportunity now to get away, and you're still trying to leave. Who are you trying to prove something to?"

"Prove something? Are you kidding me? You have no idea how hard my life has been, and how hard I have been trying to make a way to rescue you and our families together, Ray. So my life isn't just about being a Scribe, it's about glorifying God, making a way for young girls and women, and it's always, *always* been about you."

"Well, I guess that makes two of us, then." He crossed his arms. "I've waited for you, passed up beautiful women with money and real potential—"

"What am I, then, Ray?" I cut in, eyes burning, not wanting to hear about other women and money and potential.

His mouth hung open for a second and finally he cleared his throat and said, "That's not what I meant."

"I know some people look at me with my dark skin and think I'm not beautiful. I know I've dreamed bigger than Blakenberge could offer, and it's been hard to show that my dreams were worth anything. But even if I'm not beautiful, and even if my dreams seem out of reach, my potential to become anyone or anything is real." I shook my head, trying to stay calm. "I didn't know you thought I couldn't do it. I didn't know you thought I wouldn't become a Scribe."

"No, that's not what I meant. I just meant that, at the

time, when we were just merchants, I waited for you. Even when my parents wanted me to marry some other woman who was far richer than we were. But I still waited, Amana, because it wasn't your skin I was looking at, it wasn't your hair, or your face or even your figure, it was you, Amana.

"The hardworking woman who feared God and made something of herself, that's who I loved and who I waited on." He pressed his lips together. "I only said you were lost because I didn't know if you were serious about being a Scribe. I'm sorry if I offended you."

Ray squeezed my hand and then brought it to his lips. "I can't lose you again," he whispered against my skin. "I want to be with you, no matter what. So, let's return together."

I shook my head. "Ray, I can't take you."

"I know. You don't have to take me, but I'm going with you. I don't know where I'll stay, but I'm not going to let you go ever again."

"Ray," I searched my mind for words, but nothing came. Ray had always wanted to go with me, even when I'd first told him all those months ago. I'd managed to convince him to stay back then, but this time he was adamant.

I looked up from the table and said, "Can you really walk away and leave everything behind for one person? You have a whole family who loves you, Ray—you've got a new little sister now. Leaving might endanger them, or at least endanger yourself."

"What are you so afraid of? I mean, all they've done is lock you in a fancy house. What can they do to you or to me that's so bad?"

"That's just it, Ray, I don't know."

Ray sat back against the old chair and frowned. "You're not telling me something."

My palms felt slick with sweat. I swallowed and looked away.

"Amana, you've gotta tell me the truth. What are you so afraid of?"

"I did something," I finally confessed. "I stole some work from Mr. Marlowe and sent it off as my own."

Silence was thick in the air. Ray's face was calm, no hard lines or signs of anger on his visage. "How would they know it was you who stole the work?" he finally asked.

"Because they were unfinished works. No one else has access to the scribal house except for one other young man. But he only comes when he's discovered new work for Marlowe."

Ray ran a hand through his silky hair. "Ok."

"Ok?"

"Yeah, ok. I just needed to know what had you so spooked."

Now *I* was squinting. "Ain't you going to yell at me an' tell me I was stupid for doing that?"

"Hmph. Do I need to?"

I pulled back from the table and breathed deeply. Sometimes what Ray didn't say hurt more than what he would say. But even though I felt horrible, there was still some relief that he hadn't scolded me.

He asked, "When do you need to be back?"

"I was planning to leave tomorrow, after lunch. Horses are faster than donkeys, so I can leave a bit later and still arrive at a decent time. I'll have time to spare before Ben Jones and Marlowe arrive back so I can clean the place up a bit."

Ray took a deep breath, covering his face and speaking from behind his hands. "We'll pack your things once we get there and be gone by the time they show up."

"What? I can't leave, Ray. I worked so hard to get into there!" I slammed my hands on the table, frustrated that he still didn't understand.

"Amana!" he yelled back. "You're not even writing for yourself. You're not doing anything at that place. So why stay there doing nothing when you can be elsewhere actually writing?"

"You don't get it! No woman has ever been in there, I'm the *first*! I *have* to stay and become a real Scribe."

"Favian, what is wrong with you?" His voice shattered as he spoke. Immediately, I calmed down and felt bad for yelling. "You're not even writing," he muttered. "All you do is smalltime stuff that isn't even important. If you stay there, no one will ever know who Favian was. If you stay there, you die there, and no one will ever know a woman lived in that house all those months." He stood from his chair. "What you don't seem to understand is, you were a Scribe while being formed in your mother's womb. You were a Scribe before you even had consciousness. God gave you the Gift, and nothing anyone can do can take it away. Being in that house doesn't make you a Scribe, Favian, believing in God and using the Gift He entrusted to you for righteousness does." He let out a breath, like he was happy all that was finally off his chest. "You don't have to be there, but if you insist, I will go with you wherever you want to go."

Ray was right. I'd let that house define me. I never even thought I could do anything as a Scribe unless I was there. But I finally understood that I *was* a Scribe, in the scribal house or not.

"Alright," I sighed. "We leave tomorrow morning. But, Ray, are you sure you can leave everyone behind?"

He walked around to the back of my chair and placed both hands on my shoulders. "For you, I could do anything."

The next morning, Ray arrived at first light. When I saw him coming up the road, I hopped off the windowsill and went to the door.

"Good morning," he greeted me with a warm kiss on my forehead.

"Good morning," I said back. "How'd it go with the family?"

Ray took a breath and went inside with me following behind. He stood looking out the kitchen window as he spoke. "It went alright," he lied. I know Ray loved me, but to walk away from all he's known wasn't easy for him. But I admired his strength, and his dedication.

I walked over to him and pressed my head against his back. He was wearing clean clothes today and they smelled nice. He'd really decided to go with me, and I was incredibly grateful. He placed a hand on mine as I hugged him, and I felt him breathe deeply.

"Thank you, Murray."

Ray turned and hugged me tightly. He kissed the top of my head, and asked, "So, are we ready?"

"Oh!" I let go of him and ran over to the pile of clothes on the bed. "First, I have a surprise."

Ray raised an eyebrow.

"Here." I shoved the folded clothes at him.

He squinted at me, then at the clothes, and before he could speak, I said, "These are borrowed goods. But I wanted to see you wearing them."

Ray rolled his eyes. "You stole another man's clothes

and want me to wear them?"

"Exactly!" I squealed.

Ray stared at me, but he didn't speak as he moved toward the washroom.

"I just wanted to see you in something nice!" I called.

"You couldn't *buy* me something nice?"

"Just put the clothes on." I sat on the bed to rewrap my hair. As I finished my braid, Ray opened the door and stepped out.

I had never seen a suit like this before. Most suits men wore had stockings and short jackets, but this did not. Ray stepped out in long pants that stopped right above shining leather shoes. He wore a jacket that was short and crisp in the front, while a long black trail flowed behind him. The suit jacket was made of deep burgundy velvet accented with black buttons. The cuffs were gold with diamond encrusted jewels. A bow sat around his neck, and he'd pulled his hair into a bun atop his head. The clothes looked tailored for Ray, they hung so naturally on him, while accentuating his build. I sat on the bed with a hand over my mouth. A gentle blush charmed his cheeks, and he gave me a bashful smile.

"Wow," I finally managed.

Ray chuckled nervously as he held a hat under his left arm, and a cane covered in black paint with a gold ball on top in his right hand. I hadn't noticed his gloves until then, they were black with burgundy accents.

"You look amazing."

I moved from the bed to feel the fuzzy material beneath my hands. There was no way that suit was tailored for Marlowe. He would've looked so dumb in it, but Ray looked wonderful. Maybe that's why Marlowe had never worn it, he didn't like it, perhaps. Whatever the reason, I didn't care.

"I feel kind of ridiculous, honestly. Is this what the rich people wear over there?"

"Uh, no," I laughed. "I've never seen a suit like this before. It looks more expensive than gold coins alone. Maybe Marlowe was waiting to debut it for something."

"Or maybe he just didn't like it," Ray said. I nodded agreement. "Well," he stepped back, fiddling with the hat. "I'll load the horses. Be ready soon."

I nodded and dashed back into the bedroom so I could change, too. When I'd finished cramming myself into the clothes I'd brought, I went to find my fiancé.

"Ray," I called. He was still out with the horses, holding a leather bag above his head when he heard my voice. He looked up and froze.

I stood in the doorway in a floor-length dress the same burgundy color as his suit with black accents. The ruffles of the gown were trimmed in black, and the bodice had pearls sewn into it as décor. I wore a hat instead of a headwrap, letting a few of my coils peep out. It was large and had a dramatic look to it. A big black bow sat at the front, while lace and pearls decorated the rim. I wore black lace gloves to match, and face-paint for the first time in front of Ray.

"Amana?" His questioning voice made me want to run back in and take off the ridiculous clothes.

"I'm sorry, Ray. This is what most rich women wear, and I figured it would be easier for us to get across the bridge if we wore expensive clothing. Don't worry, I can change once I cross the bridge."

"No! Don't change," he breathed. "Not ever."

"Do you like it?"

He drifted off and I watched his eyes trace my figure. I cleared my throat loudly and he suddenly snapped from his imprudent trance.

"You were saying?"

"Right, you look amazing. I just didn't know you'd changed quite so much. I mean even your waist looks—"

"Alright, it's time to go." I held up a hand, refusing to listen to the inspection details. Ray smiled and offered a gloved hand as I descended the steps and neared our horses.

He smirked stupidly. "I am lost for words."

I rolled my eyes and got on my horse with him making more remarks behind me. "Are you ready now?"

"I am," Ray said.

* * *

As we rode into the city, people stopped to marvel at us. It was uncommon for a woman to ride a horse, but I had no time to buy a coach, especially not in Blakenberge. I trotted along on an albino stallion, making a statement louder than any coach ever could. As we rode through the city, women foamed at Ray, and men envied him. An albino stallion and one that was tamed was rare and more expensive than any other horse. It was Marlowe's horse, but he never rode him. Whenever I went to get fresh air, or visit the mailing center, I would stop to pet him and get to know him.

"Amana, people are staring everywhere," Ray said.

"I know, you look great."

Ray chuckled as a voice called to him. "Young man! Excuse me, young sir, but where in the world did you get such fine linen?"

"Uh," Ray slowed his horse. "It's quite fine, isn't it?"

I nearly cried laughing at him pretending to be so fancy. He was making a funny voice when he spoke.

"Why indeed it is, my lord! Where could you have gotten something like that? I have never seen such marvelous work. Do you mind if I get a closer look?"

Ray glanced at me, and I tried to subtly shake my head,

but he hopped off his horse and replied, "I don't see why not!"

A small crowd gathered; the popularity immediately went to Ray's head. Most of his life he'd been overlooked, especially with his mother having another child. And now he was wifeless, just trying to work as much as possible since he had nothing better to do. I was happy to see him happy, but too much attention could be bad, and things started to get awkward when the man said, "Now where did you say you got this from? Such beautiful material. My father is a seamstress here in this district, and I remember him working on a piece quite similar, if not the same. But surely it wasn't for you."

"Surely, you know to mind your matters!" I finally spoke. Once a week, Ben made me take etiquette classes all day, so I knew my place and how to behave if and when I ever went out in public.

"Excuse me, miss? The men are talking."

"And now *we* are talking, are we not?"

A sudden hush ran through the small crowd. I remembered my merchant training, my etiquette training, and the rude way Ben used to look down at me, and I used all I knew right here, right now.

I adjusted myself on the horse and glanced down at the man "You are a fine young man, I'm sure. So, I'm a bit surprised you would question a man of such stature as my husband and do so in such a persistent manner."

"I was only asking about the clothing, my lady," he tried to explain. "But, surely he is not of much stature if you must ride your own horse instead of traveling inside a carriage."

"I choose to do as I please, but since you seem so worried about where I ride, I guess I'll tell you a bit of business that is not yours to know. We are on our way to have a coach made to my liking." The young man stood there flushing red while Ray quietly got back onto his horse, amazed.

"Darling, we've tarried far too long here, we should go now." Ray's eyes were as big as the moon as he tipped his hat at the crowd and turned to leave.

"As you wish, my dear."

As I passed the young man, I leaned down and said, "If you must know, we would never dream of buying clothes in such a meager city. My husband's suit was made by a foreign man, in a land full of free people and wonderful style. You—nor your father—could not even *dream* of having a suit of this grandeur." I nodded at the young man, who was as red as a beet now.

Ray and I rode the rest of the way in silence, until we entered the forest.

"What was that back there?" he asked.

"*Me*? What was that back there, *Ray*!? You got caught

up in all the little compliments. Like you didn't know that suit," I looked around and whispered angrily, "is *stolen*. Why would you get off the horse!?"

"I don't know!" He shrugged sheepishly. "I got caught up, just like you said. But don't you think that last comment was pushing it?"

"Really? You want to talk about pushing it? You nearly got us caught, Ray! And I said what I said only to deter him enough to leave us alone."

"I didn't know," Ray looked away, "I didn't know you could talk like them."

"Like who?" I glanced over, noticing the embarrassed look on his face.

"Like the people here. Why don't you talk like that when you're with me?"

"Ray, it's not like that." I sighed, thinking of Ben Jones and how each one of his words felt like a little dagger stabbing me in the gut. "I don't like talking that way, but I do it when I need to. I don't need to be all high and mighty when I'm with you. You're not like these people, Ray."

"But you are, Amana. And how can I ever measure up to that?"

We rode in silence until I finally gathered the right words. "Ray, I don't care about that fancy stuff. I came back to see you, and I am marrying you. I'm not one of these people, I just live here. And living here required me to learn a few things, it's no different from being a merchant."

Ray didn't respond. He sat on his horse in that same sullen silence as the first time we rode to the city together. The only sound that could be heard was the sudden gasp I let out when we got close to the scribal house. From our distance through the woods, I could see two horses outside in the fields.

Ben Jones and Mr. Marlowe had returned.

Chapter Nine
The Scarlet Letter

"Ben and Marlowe are home!" I cried.

"Ok! So ..." Ray was just sitting there in his saddle, his eyes wide open and his mouth parted. He licked his lips as he tried to come up with a plan. "Let's just leave everything and get out of here. We don't have to get into a conflict with them."

I jumped off my horse while Ray was talking. "I've got too much here; I'm taking what's mine and then we can go. Take the horse around back and wait for me there."

"Amana!" Ray yelled as quietly as he could. When I kept walking, he jumped off his horse and ran beside me. "Would you at least listen?"

I whirled on him, turning so fast he had to take a step

back. "We've come this far, Ray! I'm getting what's mine and then I'm leaving. Besides, we need money, and—technically—as a Scribe, half of the proceeds in that house are mine, anyways."

"Now really isn't the time for specifics." Ray shook his head.

"Who's out there?" an angry voice called.

It was Marlowe. I shoved Ray away and ran into the house, quickly closing and locking the door behind me. Quiet footsteps took me through the old cabin until I came face to face with Ben Jones. His eyes widened, and he lunged at me—covering my mouth and dragging me into the room beside us.

I tried to fight, but Ben was stronger than he looked. His grip on me tightened as he whispered into my ear, "Listen to me! Marlowe is furious. I'm going let you go but you can't scream, or he'll find you."

Even if it this was a trap, there was nothing I could do besides trust Ben. This was the man who shot at me for trespassing, if he wanted to hurt me, he would have done that the moment he bumped into me.

I nodded, agreeing to stay calm and keep quiet. Slowly, Ben let go and we untangled ourselves. I was leaning against him since he'd dragged me off my feet, but as I straightened up and looked at him, I realized how awkward this whole situation was. Ben straightened his jacket and raised an eyebrow the way he always did when he had more to say but didn't want to speak it.

I frowned, not in the mood for his games. "Just spit it out."

He raised his hands defensively. "Nothing. You just look nice."

I twisted my frown into a crooked smile. I'd forgotten all about the fancy clothes and face-paint. "Thanks, Ben."

"What did you come back here for?" he asked in an angry whisper. "You were gone, you should've stayed away." There was a small bit of evening light creeping into the room, casting a shadow across his face.

"I have work here that I need, plus money and clothes. This was my home for a little while. I have things here I don't want to leave behind."

Ben sighed and covered his face with his hand. In the silence, I could hear Marlowe swearing and throwing things around upstairs.

"Why is he so angry?" I said quietly, flinching as something crashed hard right above us. Marlowe sounded more than angry—he seemed uncontrollable.

Ben folded his arms. "Let's not pretend, Favian. It's not about his play being replaced, good plays come regularly, but it's his own plays rewritten so well they're unrecognizable as his own. They only share similar names and themes." He paused, and I could tell he was looking at me, but the light behind him made his expression hard to make out.

"His ego was shattered when they upheld this new writer's wonderful work, but his heart was broken when he found the work that was so astounding—so much better than his. It was just one script at first, but this new writer has proved himself and now two scripts are being passed around, gaining momentum." He raised that eyebrow again. "But it's not the fame; it's his work, and what his work could have been. We knew instantly who framed Marlowe, but what could we say? We couldn't tell them the work was stolen and rewritten by someone we have caged in the scribal house, let alone a woman. And beyond that, to be quite frank, the work was at a level much better than anything Marlowe has ever written."

Even though Marlowe was right above me, throwing things and swearing so loudly he was scaring the devil, I felt overcome with joy. I wanted to scream to the world, to my parents who tried to hold me back, to my hometown that was so empty, and to myself. But I couldn't rejoice. I could only stand there, ashamed of the problems I'd stirred, until Ben said, "It's our fault." I looked up from my shoes and stared at him. He wasn't facing me anymore; he'd turned to stare out the open window.

"What do you mean "your fault"? I shouldn't have stolen that work. If I hadn't, none of this would be happening.

I'm sorry," I said.

He shook his head, still looking out that window. "We forced you to become someone you're not. Backed you into a corner until you decided you had to win by any means necessary ... and you have. You won a race we tried to keep you out of. You won because you didn't come here to race, you came here to participate—to work as a team. But Marlowe feared losing his place in society, and I was too much of a coward to do anything. But the deed is done now, and you must get far from here soon.

"Marlowe will come for you, but he won't go very far, in fear of his name being slandered, and being associated with a woman who claims to be a Scribe." He turned to me now, the look on his face somber, if not sad. "So, you must go now. There's no more time." He grabbed my arm and pushed me toward the window.

"Wait!" I whispered. "I'm not leaving without my other manuscripts or my money. And my wax stamper!" Ben stared at me, and I stared right back. I tried to glare as hard as I could, but, looking in his eyes, I could see how tired he was. His face and his body weren't exhausted, but his mind and his heart were.

He took a breath. "Fine, I'll go get your things. Stay here and stay quiet. If he comes in here don't make a sound and don't move until I get back. Understood?"

"Yes." I nodded.

"Get under the desk over there and stay quiet."

I ran to the desk and slid under it, gathering my big dress to pull it underneath with me. I closed my eyes and listened to Ben's footsteps walking away. As soon as the door closed behind him, I felt the world hush. I could hear my own breath, could hear my own heartbeat. It didn't register until now, as I hid under a desk with my dress bunched around me, that I was in serious trouble. I was in *danger*.

Marlowe was furious—furious enough that even Ben felt the need to help me escape. I knew it was wrong to steal, but I thought if I changed most of the scripts, it didn't qualify as stealing, or at least I'd hoped it didn't. But it was wrong nonetheless, so I cried in my heart, because I was too scared to cry aloud.

"God, please forgive me. I stole and caused all this trouble. And I don't think I ever would have asked for forgiveness if this trouble hadn't happened. I repent and beg of your forgiveness in Jesus' name, amen."

Before I could totally finish the prayer, the door flung open, and I knew it wasn't Ben. I covered my mouth, praying Marlowe would leave. But he walked around, his footsteps heavier and slower than Ben's.

"When I find you, I'm going to end you and your little career. I'll make sure no one will ever remember you." He stomped through the room and stood at the window. A creaking noise made me jump, shifting my loud dress. I clamped a hand over my mouth and held my breath. Tears pricked at the backs of my eyes. We sat in that choking silence so long, the tears swelled and rolled down my cheeks. That's when I heard a clicking sound, the cocking of a gun.

Thump! Thump! Thump!

His footsteps came closer, and I took a shaky breath. Suddenly, a loud noise went off above us and the footsteps stopped abruptly.

"Ben? What was that?"

Marlowe ran from the room, closing the door behind him. I exhaled hard as I listened to him bounding down the hall. Above the noise of his dash upstairs, I heard the window open; the creaking noise was louder this time, drawing me from under the desk.

"Amana?"

"Ray?" I whispered angrily. He pulled himself halfway into the window. "I got worried out there. So, I walked around and found this window. Thank God you happened to be here."

"Ray, that is the stupidest thing ever. You're gonna get us caught!" I snapped as quietly as I could.

"Well, help me in and we won't get caught!"

Ray flailed around, hanging halfway in the window and halfway out. I hauled myself and my stupid dress over to help, but as soon as I reached for his hand, the door opened again.

"I knew you were in here!"

Briefly, I forgot about Ray and covered my ears from the snake. A familiar hissing noise ripped through the cool evening air, cracking the silence. A hiss, a scream, a thud. The hiss came from Marlowe's gun, the scream came from me, and the thud came from Ray. He'd fallen from the window.

"Ray!" I screamed.

"I shot the wrong one."

I heard the gun cock once more and I dived to the floor. Another shot went off, but it didn't hit me. It went through the ceiling. I scrambled on the floor with my ears covered and my heart pounding. I could feel my chest near ready to burst from the tight corset, and my body covered in sweat. My face-paint was smeared onto my dress and gloves from crying so much.

My long hair dropped down my back as I took off my hat, I needed to get out of this gaudy mess if I wanted to escape, but before I could take off anything more, I heard rustling in the doorway. I crawled from the desk and saw Ben and Marlowe fighting.

"Amana! Take the bag and run!" he cried through strained breaths.

I wasted no time. Faster than I ever thought possible in

this stupid dress, I ran from the desk and squeezed by Marlowe and Ben. My eyes darted around the hallway, when I found the bag lying by the curved stairway. I snatched it up and lifted my dress so I could run, but something stopped me. Something inside.

For reasons I couldn't explain, I didn't want to leave Ben. He was such a stubborn jerk, and he'd hardly ever been nice—even tried to kill me once—but he was helping now, when it mattered most. And who knew what Marlowe would do to him after I escaped?

"Ben!" I cried as I ran back to the room. I couldn't see him anymore, but I heard them fighting. They'd fumbled and tumbled their way deeper into the room.

"Ben, please!" I shouted, but the fighting didn't stop.

I heard three loud thumps, and I cried out in response, "Ben!"

"Amana!" he shouted back, grunting with exertion. "Just go! I'll be fine!"

I wanted to stay and help but I was torn. Ben was inside fighting for his life and Ray was outside fighting for his. He'd been shot and then dropped out a window.

Without a second thought, I ran from the house.

"Goodbye, Ben," I whispered, trying to convince myself I hadn't just abandoned him.

Around the corner, I found Ray lying down, groaning in

pain. The grass beside him was bloody. It didn't take much for me to realize something was wrong.

"C'mon, Ray, we've gotta get outta here," I whispered beside him.

He groaned, but I had no time. He'd hit his head on the fall, and it was making him fuzzy. I ran to the horses and found a cart, threw my bags inside, and ran back for Ray. Hooking my arms beneath his, I dragged him toward the horses.

Ray hollered in pain, but I couldn't stop. Blood leaked onto my dress, the stains growing larger with every step. When we got to the cart, it was hard, but I had no one else to help. I kneeled off the edge of the cart, and grabbed Ray by the arms, hauling him inside with no grace at all. He screamed—worse than he'd done when I'd first started dragging him. Then he passed out, letting go of one last breath.

With him silent, I dragged and pushed him into the cart as roughly as I needed to. Then I hooked the cart up to the stallion and rode out as quickly as I could. Half a mile up the road, I stopped to change out of my bloody dress and cover Ray with a blanket from one of the bags I'd brought up with me.

I rode in silence with no real destination in mind. I just wanted to get as far away as possible. From my position on the stallion, I could still see the scribal house in the distance. I glanced over my shoulder and squinted; Marlowe stood in the window. His back was turned, so all I could see was three sparks light up the room as three loud bangs went off.

I swallowed thickly. "Ben."

My hands trembled as I clutched the reins to my horse. But they didn't shake at all when I reached into my small bag and pulled out the handgun. Without another thought, I turned back to the house.

The front door opened quietly as I peered inside. There was blood smeared on the floors and walls of the hallway. Further down, I could see Ben slumped onto the floor, his body leaning halfway out the door. I wanted to scream but I didn't know where Marlowe was. I ran over and slid down next to Ben, that's when Marlowe said, "I knew you'd come back for him."

My eyes doubled in size as I turned to face him.

"You think you can steal from me and get away with it?"

"God," I whispered.

Marlowe laughed. "This isn't punishment from God, it's punishment from me. He wants everyone to be merciful. But I want revenge. Total and complete revenge is what I—"

BANG!

I shot without blinking or flinching. Marlowe held his

chest and staggered forward. When he dropped to his knees, I shot once more, jamming a bullet into his skull. In shock, I stood there, wishing I could wake up from this bad dream. But the night went on, proving that none of this was a dream at all.

"Go, Favian," a shaky voice whispered.

I looked down and found Ben gasping for air as he tried to speak. "Ben! C'mon, we can get you help, but we gotta go now." I looked over his body. Three holes bore into him from the bullets Marlowe had fired.

"Take this and go west," he croaked.

I began to sob, watching him pant for air, drowning in his own blood. Thick red liquid poured from his mouth as he gasped.

"Please don't go," I whispered. I went to squeeze his hand and found bloody paper in it.

"Go," he rasped once more before he shook violently, his body pleading for air that never came.

I leaned back, shocked and hurt. Ben's body jerked, twisting him at an ungodly angle as he fought for his withering life. Tears gushed uncontrollably. I had never seen someone die before, so violently, so pointlessly. Then, all at once, the death throes stopped, and his lifeless hand slipped from mine into a pool of his own blood.

Chapter Ten
Who Are you?

The night Ben died; I didn't ride out west like he'd instructed. I rode back to Blakenberge, where no one would ask questions, only small whispers.

When I arrived, it was nearly time for the sun to rise. I had ridden through the night, unable to stop thinking about Ray. He had only woken up once, but he fell back out after a while of groaning and bumping around in the cart. There was a lot of blood by the time I reached town, which set me to worrying. When I finally crossed into Blakenberge, I went to the one place I swore I'd never go back to. I went home.

It'd been a while since I'd been home, and hardly ever did I even wonder about home or my parents. I enjoyed the scribal house, it was neat, clean, and updated. But I couldn't complain about my shack, even though my parents brought their own sorrow on us, they'd still tried to make our place a home. And it *was* home—after all, I'd realized I was a Scribe right in that shack, and I will forever be grateful for that.

As we rode up to the little shack, I hopped off the horse and ran to the door, pounding so hard, I nearly broke it down.

"I'm coming! Who is it?" It was father's voice. I hadn't heard it in nearly two years since he became bedridden.

When he opened the door, he just stood there staring. I'm sure he was shocked to see me of all people, but also shocked to see me covered in dried blood.

"Amana?" he said, confused.

"Amana!?" I heard Ma rush to the door. She ripped it wide open, and then stood there just as baffled as Pa.

I swallowed hard and said, "Please, Ray's been hurt really bad; he's bleeding out in the cart. I tried to apply pressure but there's so much blood, I don't know if he'll survive!" I burst into tears.

"No crying, Amana! I need your head thinking and your hands moving if you wanna save this boy's life." Ma started rolling up her sleeves, watching me closely as she did so. Her eyes were full of judgement, as if I were to blame for this. Or maybe they weren't being judgmental at all, maybe—deep down—I knew this *was* all my fault.

Ray was hurt, Ben was dead, and I'd killed a man; all because of my own selfishness. All because I'd let my passion get the best of me and stole someone else's work. It didn't matter the motivation; if I had done what was right when I'd had the chance, Ray would be alright, and Ben would be alive.

"Amana, you hear me, girl? You're drifting. Now, come on!" Pa was shouting, his voice loud and strong for a man who'd been bedridden for what seemed like ever. He pointed at Ma and shouted, "Adella, put some water on and get some wet towels right away!"

Ma sprang into action before I did, running to grab the supplies while I stood there dumbfounded. I blinked at them, watching in awe as my parents went to work without question, without anger, without even wondering what'd happened or where I'd been. They were still my family—but it took a tragedy for me to realize that.

"Amana!" Pa's voice cracked like a whip, and I jumped, turning to run out to the cart.

Ray was lying on the floor, shivering. His color had faded, and he looked ill, worse than how Pa used to look. I wanted to cry again, but tears would do me no good. They didn't save Ben; they wouldn't save Ray now.

"Alright now, baby girl," Pa said, leaning over the cart. His face was hard as he stared down at Ray, lines and creases forming his elderly visage. A layer of sweat dampened his brow, he wiped it away with a dirty sleeve as he said, "He's still breathing, but just barely. We gotta move, and when we do, it's probably gon' hurt him." He turned to me; his eyes soft—almost gentle. It was an odd look on my father, so much emotion in those glowing orbs, like he knew this was important not just because it was Ray lying there, but because it was someone I loved. "It'll hurt," he said again. "But we gotta do it anyway. Now get up on the cart and get ya' hands under his pits. I'll grab his feet. We gon' bring him in quick-fast."

"But what about the neighbors? They'll hear him. What about his parents? They're only a few shacks down."

"That don't matter." He shook his head. "If they hear him screaming and come looking, we'll think of something, but this boy's life is in danger, we gotta save him *now*."

I nodded and climbed into the cart to stand behind Ray. He groaned softly as I got my arms under him.

"Ray, we're home," I whispered. "Pa's gonna help you, ok? Remember my grandma was a nurse? He grew up learning medical stuff from her, but we gotta move you again and it's gonna hurt."

Ray worked his mouth like he wanted to say something but only a painful moan slipped between his lips. I looked him over, taking in his damp hair, wet with sweat and stained red from blood. It was dried onto his clothes and crusted on his skin. There was so much of it, I didn't know how he was still alive in the first place. *Lord, save him*, I pleaded inside.

"On three," Pa instructed, grabbing Ray's feet. He waited for me to secure my grip before he started the countdown. "One. Two. Three. LIFT!"

Ray cried out—one sharp scream that rang in my ears, shook me in my bones. It traveled all through me, buzzing over my skin. Every hair on my body raised; I nearly dropped him, but Pa's words kept me stable.

"You gotta hold him, Amana! It'll be worse if you drop him! Now, watch your step!"

"Put me down!" Ray screamed, horror lacing his tongue. "Please! I'm begging!"

He flailed in our grip, but it was weak, like a child kicking at his parents. It wasn't the fightin' that got to me; I grunted and tugged as I followed Pa, ignoring Ray's kicks and thrashing. It was the terrible cries. Shouts of pain and tearful pleading, like a wounded animal deep in the woods—its ghostly cries echoing around you, haunting your nightmares. Tears filled my eyes as they poured from his, but I couldn't let go. If I dropped him, we wouldn't get the chance to pick him up again. He wouldn't survive a second attempt. I had to keep moving.

Stepping down from the cart was the worst. The impact

made Ray scream in a piercingly terrible noise; I wanted to cover my ears. But that was the last of it. He let out one final cry, twisting around so he could look me in the eye as he whispered something I couldn't hear. Then he let go, exhaling his will as he fell limp in my arms. He'd passed out cold.

"C'mon! Get him inside!" Pa shouted, taking advantage of his unconsciousness.

I nodded and moved with quickness, wondering what Ray had whispered.

There was a rush of movement through the shack. Ma running back and forth with towels and hot water; Pa had to find his medical kit while I sat there stroking Ray's hair, replaying the scene in my head. What had he whispered? Was it a message? One final plea to let go? A tearful goodbye?

Pa nudged me when he came over with his medical kit. He tore Ray's clothes off and barked out orders when he needed help. I tried to keep up, but I was as useless to Pa with his nursing as I was to Ma and her sewing.

Long before I was born, my father helped my grandmother when she retired from the military nursing unit. It happened when Grandpa was shot by a policeman. He was innocent, but he was also dark, and sometimes that's the same as being guilty. My grandmother was old and shaky by then; and there wasn't a good hospital willing to treat folks like my grandparents. So, my father stepped in, doing everything his ma had taught him over the years so he could save his father's life.

It was that horrible event that inspired my grandmother to open her home to anyone who'd been hurt or injured the same way her husband had. She treated people in her own living room, dark bodies lining the floor with gunshots or knife wounds or sick with disease. The hospitals turned too many of our folks away, but grandma welcomed everyone. My Pa was just a young man at the time, but he stayed by his mother's side, learning and helping however he could. It was his helping hand, and their faith in God, that got my grandfather back on his feet again. According to old stories, my Pa met Ma when she came to their house for a simple checkup. A year later, he put a ring on her finger, and they started a life together.

I could see Pa's old self coming back as he worked on Ray now. Images of the young man I've never met flashed in my head as he poured water all over Ray's bloody body to find the bullet hole.

"There." He pointed to a little hole in Ray's chest. "It didn't go through, but it's in that muscle good an' tight."

My hands began to tremble, my heart pounded in my ears, and tears made everything blurry. I wanted to speak but my mouth was suddenly dry and my jaw suddenly locked. I clenched my chest and tried to control my breathing. *Ma hates heavy breathing. Ma hates when I can't control myself.*

My anxiety made her angry because it took her back to her own darkness. If I couldn't control myself, she might slip again. But I couldn't get a grip. I couldn't even think. *What time is it? I killed a man, didn't I? Why have I been so calm about killing a man? Oh no, Ben! I should've taken his place. I should've taken Ray's place. This is all my fault. This is all my fault!* I grabbed my head as the thoughts swirled louder and louder, drowning out the fuss in the house. I couldn't breathe. *I'm trying, Ma,* I thought. *I'm trying to control myself!*

I flung myself to the floor and covered my face, screaming from behind my hands, "Please don't hit me, Mama! I'm sorry! This is all my fault! Please don't hit me!"

I stared at the floor, trying to steel myself, trying to hold onto some sense of reality. But everything was blurry, and I still couldn't breathe and now I couldn't hear, and my vision was hazy from all the tears. I curled up and rocked back and forth, muttering to myself, "Please, Ma, I'll do better. This is my fault. Give me a chance and I'll fix it." Over and over, I muttered the same words, trying to believe them, trying to convince Ma that I would do better.

Suddenly, I felt someone touch my shoulder, but I flinched away. Through the blurriness, I could make out my father's form. "Amana, come on now," he spoke softly as he reached out to touch me, but I screamed, "Don't touch me!"

I saw his hand immediately stop and I heard him ask Ma, "What did you do to her?"

Blurriness turned to **darkness**. I let it consume me, falling into the abyss of fear and anxiety. Sitting in that void, I screamed and cried until my lungs went raw and my throat went hoarse.

There was nothing but shadows surrounding me. I was alone. I was afraid. I was going to stay in this chasm for the rest of my life. Then I felt a warmth on my back, and I knew Ma was there to kill me. But this time I would fight even if I was trapped in the dark. I would fight.

"Don't touch me!" I yelled, pulling away from the warmth, wondering which direction I would turn to find her. Everything around me was black. This was the madness my mother had lived in for too long. Her sickness had gotten hold of me, held me in place, and it would never let me go. I was mad now. Gone. Lost.

The darkness moved around me, like it was alive. I felt faint, like it was time to give up. With the strength of a babe, I swung my fist into the shadows, trying to fight enemies I knew weren't there. They were all in my head. But this darkness was real. It was all around me, until I turned and found someone standing right before me.

"In Me, there is no darkness, only light." A hand reached out through the darkness and touched my head. As soon as it made contact, the shadows peeled away to reveal a world bursting with light.

"Where am I?"

"I brought you here for a moment. I saw you in a lot of turmoil," the man before me said.

"Who are you?" I blinked. If I wasn't crazy before, I was truly mad now.

The man smiled and said, "Who do you say I am?"

Realization hit me. I knew those words, had read them even though I wasn't supposed to. *That* part of the Book was off limits to women. I stared at the smiling man. His face radiant and pouring love from his smile. His eyes took you to a world of their own with just one glance, and his skin poured out pureness and mercy. He was emitting light from his entire being, and for a split second, as I looked in the man's eyes, I could see his beaten and battered face with a crown of thorns crushed onto his head.

I gasped and covered my mouth. "You are the Christ, Son of the living God."

"Blessed are you, Favian Amana Hart! For flesh and blood has not revealed this to you," I spoke with Him, and in unison we said, "but my Father who is in heaven."

"That's from the Bible! I remember! You're Jesus!" I exclaimed. He smiled more brightly when I recognized Him. But suddenly I felt an urge to fall before Him. "Please forgive me. I have sinned and lied and I stole work that caused all this trouble. Please take me, not Ray!" I began to cry again, tears poured down as I knelt before him. I wept uncontrollably, letting my tears soak His feet in my sorrow.

"Stand up, Favian, I do not know what you speak of. My blood has washed away every sin, and we never remember it. The consequences of sin are not remembered as consequences to us, but we only see you learning how to trust God in every situation. All have sinned, but *all* can be forgiven. Cry no more, Favian, for I have forgiven you, and I no longer remember your sin. Now stand, my beloved one, it is not time for you or Murray to meet my Father yet.

"There is much work to be done, much liberation to be brought to my daughters of the Earth, and you have been chosen to do so. Murray will recover quickly, I have anointed your father's hands, and will send angels to tend to him when your father is finished. Now stand."

The command was strong enough to bring me to my feet. His beautiful hand reached out and wiped away my tears. "I will wipe away every tear from you, and you *will* bring glory to my Father's name. I am sending you where no man can stop you. Have no fear, Favian, believe in me and trust my Father. We will not forsake you, for my Father's Holy Spirit lives in you now, and you will not fail."

I was lost for words. Jesus stood before me, reassuring

all that I thought was a lost cause. I thought I had disappointed Him, and even strayed away, but there before Him, I learned that He had never stopped loving me and had never condemned me.

"It's time for you to go now, Favian."

"Wait, what happened to me? I don't remember."

"Your stress took you deep within yourself, but I am bringing you back. Now, when you go back, rest for three full days, then start working on your scripts. Shakespeare will be remembered. But you can no longer walk with heavy feet. Go freely and swiftly. Know that I am with you and that I love you."

He wrapped His arms around me, and warmth filled my body. Abruptly, the warmth grew cold, and air gushed around me. As I flew through the air, I could see Jesus parting the darkness, making everything into light. I was sucked into a tunnel of light and traveled quickly back to Earth.

I could see my body lying in bed, and as I rushed toward it, I heard Jesus speaking to me, "Forgive your parents as I have forgiven you and them. You will need the kindness I have bestowed upon their hearts that they may help you as much as you need."

And with that, I was dropped into my body. I sat up quickly, gasping for air.

Chapter Eleven
Without A Trace

Just as Jesus instructed, I rested for three full days. I stayed in bed, and only left to go to the bathroom. I didn't visit Ray or see anyone else, but my parents made frequent trips to my room. They brought me food and water regularly ... well, *Pa* brought me food and water regularly. Ma was still having a tough time facing me after what'd happened, but whenever she came in, I greeted her with the same smile I did Pa.

I practiced forgiving my parents in my heart. I didn't know I'd been so angry with them until Jesus told me to forgive them. There were times in the scribal house when I felt alone; I blamed my parents for that—for making me run away from them. There were times when I was angry at them for even trying to stop me. I felt like maybe things would've been easier if I'd been able to get to the scribal house sooner. Or maybe they wouldn't have. I suppose I'll never know for certain.

Sitting in bed, nursing my mind and body, I prayed often—every single day—reminding myself to forgive my parents. I tried not to think about what happened to Ray or what transpired in the house. No one except Ben Jones knew I'd killed Mr. Marlowe. But Ben Jones was dead now. So, I was the only one with that horrible secret and the guilt that came with it. I didn't want it to torment me, so I would think of other things to keep my mind busy, like new plays.

When I finally got out of bed, I followed the second part of the instructions I'd been given and immediately got back to work. I wrote script copies all day, barely eating, mostly just writing. I couldn't bring myself to go see Ray. Pa said he was doing better every day; he'd never seen such a fast recovery. I chose not to tell him why Ray was recovering so well and so fast, but I was happy for him, nonetheless.

Pa told me he could stay awake for much longer now—even said he'd asked about me on day three and four. But I wasn't ready to see Ray. I was afraid that all the memories from that night would flood back, and I feared another psychotic crack. I didn't want either of those to happen, so I kept to myself and remained in my room until I felt strong enough to handle a reunion.

After nearly two weeks of recovery, I brought myself to Ray's door. At first, I just stood outside of it, breathing deeply. He'd been staying in my parents' room while they slept in the living room. Pa said Ray needed a bed; lying on a hard floor might make things worse if he got uncomfortable and tried to move. I didn't argue with him. But as I stood outside the door, I wondered how the room looked. I hadn't been inside for so long ... even before all this, back when Pa was always restin' in there 'cause he'd been so sick.

I raised my fist and knocked, hoping Ray was asleep, but he wasn't.

"Come in," he answered.

Nervously, I pushed open the door and found Ray sitting up in bed. His shirt was off, and his hair pulled back. His chest was bruised with black, blue, and green spots and a deep redness surrounded the white patch adhered to his chest. When our eyes met, I felt like vomiting. I wanted to give him an excuse for why I hadn't come to visit but standing there before him made me question the validity of my excuse. Instead, the first thing I did was offer an apology.

"I'm sorry," I said coldly. Ray had looked away by now. He didn't say anything for a while.

Just when I'd begun to wonder if he'd heard me, he opened his mouth and said, "Your father told me what happened. About how you broke down. I'm sorry I couldn't help you, Amana."

Confusion washed over me at the sound of his words. Ray had apologized to me. I couldn't understand how or why he could feel any of this was his fault.

I blurted, "Don't apologize! How could any of this be your fault? I'm the one to blame. If I hadn't stolen those plays, or even wanted to be a Scribe, I could've thought more rationally. But I was so focused on myself, I put both our lives in danger, and you ended up paying the cost."

"That's not true!" he yelled. His tone shocked me into a stiff silence. I wasn't sure if he was angry or upset or sad or what. "If I hadn't climbed through the window," he continued, voice shaky. "If I had just stayed outside. Or if I had just trusted you for a *second*, we wouldn't be in this situation. I deserved everything that happened to me. I'm—"

"Stop it." I couldn't take any more. "What is this? Some kind of nobility trip? You didn't deserve to be shot or fall from a window and hit your head. It's my fault, so just let me accept responsibility for once!" I was yelling now, fists balled and fingernails digging into my palms. I wanted to punch something. I was angry and sad and scared all at once.

"I can't let you blame yourself like that," Ray said.

It was silent for a moment as we gazed at each other. Then, without notice, Ray offered me the smallest smile I'd ever seen—just the corner of his mouth upturned so his face was distorted by a goofy grin. I chuckled, letting go of a breath I hadn't known I'd been holding. Then Ray chuckled too and suddenly that quiet room that'd been filled with sickness and rage and sorrow for so long, was filled with laughter.

"Look at us," he said, catching my eye. He was smiling, fully smiling like none of this had happened. Like he wasn't recovering from a gunshot wound.

"I know," I said. I took my first step into that room in years and closed the door behind me. Ray beckoned for me to join him, so I sat on the bed beside him, leaned my head against his shoulder, and said, "We were both trying to be so nice."

He chuckled, his shoulder moving slightly up and down. "Let's both take the blame."

"Agreed."

We sat there like that for a while. His arm was too weak to hug me, so I kept my head on his shoulder, enjoying the familiar smell of his skin. As we sat there, Ben's face flickered in my memory. I immediately tried to swallow the image and the pain that came with it, but an alarm went off inside me. Suddenly, I remembered the paper he'd passed to me before he'd died.

I sat up with a gasp, making Ray wince in response.

"What's wrong?" he asked.

"I just remembered; Ben gave me a piece of paper before—" I trailed off.

"Before what?" Ray nudged me.

"Ray," I whispered. I wanted to cry but I had run out of tears.

"What?" he whispered back playfully. It dawned on me, at the sight of his silly grin and the way he looked at me like there was nothing wrong and no reason to be upset ... Ray didn't know. He had no clue what'd happened after he'd been shot. He didn't know that Ben was dead and that I was to blame. He didn't know I'd killed a man.

"I have to go to the outer banks of the city," I said, turning away. "Out near the river—to get rid of that handgun."

"Why?" His voice switched from playful to concerned.

"Ben was shot and killed by Marlowe."

Ray didn't say anything for a while. Neither did I. I'd wanted to keep this secret of mine just that, a secret. But I was worried if anyone started looking for Marlowe, their inquiries might make it back to Ray and he might start to wonder, too. Ray didn't have the Gift. He could speak two languages and he could make out common words and letters most everyone knew, but he wasn't special like me.

I'd let that fool me, let it blind me to the fact that not having the Gift didn't make you stupid. Ray would have put the pieces together. He would have figured things out. It was better to confess now than later.

I took a breath and said the words. "I killed Marlowe."

The truth hung in the air for a minute. It was sour—it stank, like a wet rag left out too long. I was a killer. But, for the first time, I took comfort in my place in this world as a woman. If Ray turned me in, I wouldn't be a killer, I'd be a *murderess*. And that was different. That was killin' done at the hands of an innocent lady—it was nearly unheard of, if not thought impossible by some. I may have been guilty, but at least I was a guilty woman. Because a woman wouldn't get as much time as a man. A woman wouldn't be taken seriously. So, when it all came undone, I'd rather be a murderess than a murderer.

More confident now, I filled the lingering silence with the rest of my confession. "I shot Marlowe with his own gun. Right in the chest. And when he fell to his knees, I shot him again, without hesitation. That shot went right through the center of his forehead."

Ray looked uncomfortable. Not judgmental, but more fearful and worried than I'd ever seen him before. He asked me, "How did it feel?"

I was puzzled. I tried to find the words to answer him, but he kept talking. "Never mind. I don't want you to go back to that place in your head. But ..." he seemed to ponder a moment, chewing on the words. "Why'd you do it?" He shook his head. "I guess I shouldn't ask that, either."

"It was me or him," I replied. "He had his own gun aimed right at me. I just shot before he did. I shot a second time because I was so angry. It was like that one bullet pinned all of my emotions right onto Marlowe. I felt ... relieved." Ray didn't say anything. He just sat there quietly, staring at the floor.

I was beginning to feel uncomfortable when he finally said, "Keep the gun."

My head jerked up as I looked over at him, but he wouldn't meet my gaze.

"It was your mother who rescued my father," he said, staring straight ahead at nothing at all. "When I was a child, my father accidentally killed a man. Your mother's father was a gunsmith before he died. She took that gun to him and had the barrel changed. The murder weapon was never found, and the case went cold. You have to do the same."

"My grandfather is dead," I said.

"Ask your mother. I know she'll know someone."

"But what if they can't do it? What if they start asking questions?"

Ray grunted. "If you're too afraid, then we'll come up with a different plan."

"It's not that, I just—"

The door pushed open to reveal Ma standing there. Her brows were low, and her eyes were intense. For a moment fear jolted through me and I looked away.

"I'll do it," she spoke softly. Mother's voice was always hard and coarse, but in that moment, it was as soft as snow.

"What are you talking about?" I said nervously.

Ma stepped into the room. "I've caused you so much pain, so please," tears swelled in her eyes, "let me do this for you. I know it can't make up for everything, but it can be a start. Just let me do this."

"Ma," I said. I extended my arms to her. She hesitated for a moment, and then lunged into them, whimpering an apology into my chest. I glanced over at Ray; he gave me a nod.

"Ma," I said, pulling away. "You don't owe me nothin'. But, if you say you can do this, I'll let you."

"I know a man." She wiped away her tears. "He's a good friend of my father. He and his son still work in the business. I can get them to do it."

"Will they change the barrel for us?" Ray asked.

"Yes, and they'll sell the old one to a scrapper."

"What will the scrapper do, then?" I asked.

"They'll get it into a foundry, and it'll be history after that."

"But," Ma looked over at Ray while he spoke. "What if the scrapper doesn't get it there? What will the foundry even do with it?"

"A job like this is given to specific scrappers, one who works directly for the foundry. They take metal from different places, and they'll bring it to the foundry to be melted down and used for something that doesn't need only one type of metal. I know the scrapper they'll give it to.

"He'll be the same one that rescued your father, Ray. We can trust them, so don't worry about it anymore. If you do, you'll bring suspicion on yourselves."

Ray was silent, sitting on the bed. I knew he was a little worried—I was worried, too. But we had no choice.

"Thank you, Ma. I appreciate all of this."

Ma reached out her big, wide hands and gently held my face. "Thank you for coming back." She kissed my head and left the room.

"Well, I guess I better go get her the gun, then."

Ray nodded.

"Ray, I need you to be ok with this. It was your plan, anyway."

"I know. I just didn't realize how much risk would be in it. And now your mother knows you've killed someone."

"Yeah." I scratched my head and sighed. "We need some privacy of our own."

"Agreed," Ray said.

I turned to leave but stopped at the door, a memory blooming in my head. "Wait. Ben told me to go west before he died," I said, turning back toward him.

"Ok, but how far west? Those aren't very good instructions," Ray criticized.

"The man was dying, Ray, he could barely speak. Give him a break." I palmed the back of my neck. "I haven't even gone through the bag he left me or the note, either."

"He left you a note?"

"Yes. I have to go, Ray, I'll be back."

"Wait, Amana—" I closed the door and rushed to my bedroom. Pa had brought the bags in a few days ago, but I'd never checked them.

I remember when I took the letter, I didn't have anywhere to put it until I got back to the horses. I searched frantically, until I found the note in the satchel holding the gun. I exhaled, relieved I hadn't lost it. I wanted to open it, but there was so much else I needed to do first, so I put the bloody letter under my pillow.

"I'll take this to Ma." I grabbed the satchel with the gun and left the room. "Ma!" I called.

"Yes?" She emerged from the living room holding a tray of drinks.

"Here." I held out the satchel. Her eyes widened and we exchanged the drinks and the satchel.

"I'll go right now."

"Thanks again, Ma."
She nodded and left.

Chapter Twelve
We're NOT Who We Say We Are ... Are We?

After Ma took the gun, I holed myself up in my room until I finished copying the scripts. It took me three days to finish enough copies for both churches. I'd found a mailing center in the small town between Blakenberge and Sesame. I took the script copies there, as well as a few copies of Romeo and Juliet.

"Does he write them all himself?" a woman at the mailing center asked. I was confused for a moment, then I finally realized the "he" she was talking about was me.

"Oh! You mean Shakespeare? Of course; he has no one else to help him, so he just writes when he can."

"He must live in the mountains. Printing presses haven't made it up there yet. Poor guy."

"I forgot about the presses." I placed my hand on my forehead and sighed. Suddenly, I remembered I was only Shakespeare's *assistant* out in public. The woman looked confused, so I said, "He was just talking to me about finding other options."

"How would a poor girl like you know much about a printing press?" she asked, eyebrows furrowed.

"I don't! I've only seen one once. Just to uh, look, I guess. I was on a trip for something else and I wandered inside ... kinda."

The woman rolled her eyes and said, "Well, if he has more to write, we've got a pressing machine in the back that a few people know how to work. Tell him to have you drop off a play to us, and we can have copies mailed out for him."

"That's excellent! How much does it cost to print?"

She looked me up and down, scrutinizing every part of me. "I figured he must be wealthy since he has such a well-dressed servant girl like you running his errands." She paused for a moment, as if a candle was suddenly lit in her head. "A man that wealthy and that brilliant would do well at the Scribal School. He obviously has his reasons for not attending, still, I wonder how he's gone unnoticed for so long. It does seem a bit odd that he emerged with no scribal help at all. Really makes you question the Gift."

"Ahh." I looked away, feeling the muscles in my back

knot up from all my nerves going crazy. This lady was asking too many questions, making too many comments I couldn't reply to. "You know, he never talks much of his past or reasoning for his decisions. He just works."

"Right," she said, eyebrow raised. "Well, I'm sure he talks of it, just not to his servant girl." Then she cackled like that was hilarious. Just to let go of the breath I'd been holding, I chuckled, too. *If only you knew.*

"Printing is expensive, girl," the woman went on. "A gold callios can get you five pages, but for Shakespeare, we can up the pages a bit."

I smiled. I was a Scribe now, but I was a merchant at heart. "Well, Shakespeare is a growing name, having your press associated with him would bring you a lot of business."

The woman squinted and said, "True, but he is *only* growing."

"He moved Marlowe's plays right off their thrown," I said casually.

The woman's eyes opened wide. "Really?"

"Yes! Churches and theatres are gonna start performing his plays instead of Marlowe's."

She covered her mouth, eyes darting around the room as if she could find the truth somewhere inside. I shrugged my shoulders when her shocked gaze landed on me again. "Well, in that case, we can do a gold callios per ten pages."

Ten was the number I wanted, but I wanted to see how high I could go, so I said, "Ten is alright. But Shakespeare works on a lot of projects. I mean, I'm sure you haven't seen many gold callios. To just give them out like they're candy to print such fine work?" I stopped and shook my head. "Seems a little low to me. Let's face it, there's not much business here at your mailing center, or printing press for that matter. Let alone this entire little bridging town. Don't you want people to stop here more often instead of selling to the same people? It gets old, I bet. But," I held up a finger and she stared at it, "Shakespeare's work is valuable, plus he'll be frequenting you regularly. I think this deal could be shifted a bit, don't you? Your printing press will get more attraction, people will come here regularly, hoping to get a glimpse at the mysterious man. You'll be doing your entire town a favor and so will Shakespeare."

"You're right," she said, smiling.

"I know. So let's just say, uh, one gold callios per *copy*."

She looked at me like I was crazy, but I spoke before she could protest. "We are talking *Shakespeare*, here. You'll be the first to read his work—all the new scripts—before anyone else."

She thought for moment and finally said, "Alright then. But on one condition."

I saw this coming a mile away. To intimidate her *and*

remind her who had the higher ground, I said, "Fine. But *only* one condition, so make it good."

She swallowed, suddenly nervous, suddenly second guessing the value of this condition. "We have to meet Shakespeare."

"Condition denied."

Her face wrinkled in anger.

"Shakespeare meets no one," I said, casually straightening out the wrinkles in my dress. "He works and that's that. If he's out meeting everyone, he'll never get his work done." She looked around nervously, and since the deal was going so good, I told her, "But here's a more reasonable condition we can agree upon. Shakespeare moves often, change of scenery helps him get new ideas. But I can convince him to stay a bit longer and get you a fresh script, maybe even two."

The woman squealed, not realizing I'd already promised her this in a roundabout way. She extended a pale hand to me. "Deal."

The amount of air swirling through her head must be massive, I thought.

"Take this instead." I pulled a small piece of paper from my bag; one I'd practiced my wax seal on.

The woman took the paper and stared at it. "Whose seal is this?"

"Shakespeare's."

"Why is it an A and not an S?"

"Well, he writes for his wife, so he put her initial on the seal."

She stared at it awhile, and finally, bought the lie I'd practiced numerous times in my head. "He has a wife." She looked saddened but took the seal anyway.

"Yep," I said plainly. Then I turned toward the door. "Well, I'll be seeing you soon."

* * *

When I returned home, Ray was sitting at the wooden table reading over my new script, 'Hamlet.' This story was born from the shot I took at Marlowe and a ghost idea Ray came up with without even knowing it. I'd told him I wanted to start a new script, but I didn't know what to write. Ray jokingly said that the ghost of all the women I was supposed to use my writing to rescue would haunt me if I didn't come up with a good story. So, I combined the ghost, with a confused man who sought revenge, and the person he sought revenge on stemmed from Marlowe.

I've never been confused on what I should be doing, but I can't deny that second shot I fired was definitely a shot of revenge. I felt like this story allowed me to somehow confess to my crimes through the drama of the characters. If people liked it, then I believed all would be forgiven, even though I knew God had already forgiven me. I just couldn't shake the feeling of wanting to be forgiven by others, too. So I started with Ray, the one whose forgiveness mattered most.

"It was really good." Ray smiled as I sat down across from him. His chest was healing well, and he was starting to look better, too. "You've really been working hard, Amana."

I nodded, feeling relieved that he liked the story. "Thanks, Ray. I'm really trying to make a name for myself." I paused. "For *us*."

Ray's smile widened and he reached for my hand across the table. "Amana—"

"Excuse me."

Ray and I both jumped. Ma's sudden appearance spooked us both. "Ma!" I exclaimed, almost reflexively. "I didn't notice you there."

She laughed. A hearty laugh, burly, like the big woman she was. "You lovers are loving in my kitchen." She made a face, one that made me laugh and ease some of the anxiety that'd flooded the room at her surprise entrance. "I just wanted to tell y'all I got word from the scrapper that the barrel was picked up by the foundry yesterday and should be gone by this evening, no later."

I glanced around the room, anxiety swelling all over again. For some reason, covering this crime seemed wrong, but I feared prison or dying at the stake way more.

Ray said, "Thanks, Mrs. Hart. We really don't know what we would've done if you hadn't stepped in."

"I'm glad I could help."

"Thanks, Ma," I croaked awkwardly.

Ma came over and patted my back. She said, "Now, Amana don't keep this on your mind. You keep working on them things you write on the fancy papers. Ain't nobody gonna know." I simply nodded and Ma headed for the door. "Now, I'm going to get some fresh vegetables; you guys watch the shack until I come back from the market—or your father comes back from working the stall. Y'all hear me?"

"Yes, Ma," I said.

When Ma was gone, Ray and I sat in silence for a while. It had been a minute since we'd been alone together. I fiddled with my satchel and pulled out the bloody note from Ben.

"What's that?" Ray asked.

"It's the note from Ben. I didn't want to read it alone, but we haven't had any time to ourselves yet, so I waited."

He moved from his side of the table to mine and wrapped his good arm around me. "I'm ready when you are."

I exhaled and opened the letter.

Dear Amana,

*If you're reading this, that means I didn't make it. I began writing this letter the day Marlowe and I left town. I felt so uneasy, and I knew time was short. Marlowe must always have his way, but for once in his life, he couldn't have it … **thanks** to you. The last time I saw you, I hoped it wouldn't be our last time together. There was so much more I wanted to show you, teach you, even experience with you. But I decided in my heart that this was my last chance to make things right. In doing so, I knew I'd pay the ultimate price by going against Marlowe. But I found your skill worth every risk and consequence. You **are** special Amana. Although there's much for you to learn, you are more important to the scribal progression than you know. Ahh, how I wish so desperately that I could have been there to see you become a real Scribe. I want to apologize to you, for holding you back for so long. I'm so sorry for everything, Amana. A million times over, I'm sorry.*

*I should tell you I've hated myself for a long time now. Not because I didn't have the Gift, but because I have allowed people I **knew** had the Gift to be squandered or worse, killed. But this time, Amana, I can't let that happen. I don't want it to. The first time I did nothing, I lost a friend, the next time two people were killed. Now an entire school of boys more capable than I or Marlowe could ever be, have been trapped in a situation where there is no growth. Kind of like what we did to you.*

You see, Marlowe has been a Scribe for a very long time. Story has it, he was one of the youngest men to be discovered as a Scribe at the terribly young age of four. He was extremely smart, the smartest to ever emerge. He could read and telltales of his own free will, so naturally, he seemed to have been older than his age. The Gift only grew more potent with age for him.

When Marlowe was thirty-six, a new Scribe was discovered. He was my friend, Hemmindale. We both went into the scribal school; of course, I had no Gift, but I was smart. Hemmindale, however, most certainly had the Gift. He could hold a conversation in various languages so easily with our teachers. He had handwriting so beautiful it put Marlowe's to shame. It seemed like every time a new Scribe was born, their abilities were more enhanced than the one before them. And they each were destined to do something grand with the Gift. Marlowe was to encourage with the Gift. Push those in society without it to strive for a higher literary sense. Hemmindale was to unite with the Gift. His way with words were supposed to be used to bring the people together. And you? You are meant to inspire with the Gift. Give people a reason to believe in God.

But Marlowe broke that chain of destinies.

Hemmindale was only three years older than Marlowe at the time of his discovery, he was immediately taken off to live with Marlowe. Every Scribe got an assistant, and the assistant is always the next best person at the scribal school—with capability to become a Scribe if only they had the Gift. That person was me. So,

I was sent to live with Hemmindale and Marlowe two weeks after Hemmindale left. I was excited to go because I would be Hemmindale's personal assistant, as well as his closest friend. But when I arrived, I found Hemmindale with bruises all over him.

No one ever checked in on us. Marlowe's assistant ran errands most days; he was never really around like I was for you. With no one there, Hemmindale suffered. Some nights, he was beaten endlessly. The number of times I cleaned up blood was more than I can remember.

Marlowe hated Hemmindale. He didn't want anyone to be better than him, he didn't want anyone to surpass him.

Hemmindale was obedient, despite the beatings. He loved writing with every breath in him. He continued to write even though the abuse went on for a very long time.

One day, Hemmindale left against Marlowe's wishes, bearing light bruises on his skin. He sat in the park and read aloud a story he'd written. People marveled at the young boy, but not just for the tale he told, but for the fading bruises he bore. When Marlowe and his assistant and I all arrived at the park, questions were tossed around. They wondered what'd happened to the Gifted child.

Marlowe lied.

He told them his assistant had beaten Hemmindale. He told them how he'd tried to intervene, but he was too weak and couldn't protect the child. The crowd grew wildly upset and we slipped away, leaving the assistant behind. Two weeks later, we got news that Marlowe's assistant was crushed by stones for touching a

Gifted child.

I was the last child to ever be picked as an assistant. The assistant program was demolished at the wishes of Marlowe. He said it was better just for those who are Gifted to be together, outsiders wouldn't understand. It was bittersweet that they allowed me to stay, because a year later, I witnessed something I could never forget.

On my fourteenth birthday, Marlowe broke Hemmindale's fingers. Hemmindale's writing was beginning to upstage Marlowe's— despite his tender age. Marlowe couldn't handle it, so he took his anger out on my friend. He tied him to a chair and blindfolded him. The screams and cries from Hemmindale went on all morning. I could hardly take it. Finally, Hemmindale passed out from exhaustion and pain. But it wasn't enough for Marlowe.

"Fingers will heal," he'd murmured as he stood over Hem's limp body. "But a brain won't."

*That day, I ran through the woods carrying what I thought was a lifeless body. I had to find help, and I ran as fast as I could while my friend bled out. That day, God worked a miracle. A woman heard my desperate cries. She was able to help us, and Hemmindale survived. But when he woke up, he had nearly no recollection of where he was or even his own name. That was when **I** began to lie. The woman asked if the beaten boy was the Scribe; I told her that he was my assistant, and I was the Scribe. She asked me where the boy was from, and I told her Blakenberge, because I used to live* *there. In that moment I became someone I was not. Posh, uppity, tightlipped. I became that way because I wasn't living for myself anymore. I was living for the Gift.*

*I told the woman that day that his name was Hemmindale, but that was a lie, too. **My** name—my real name—is Hemmindale, and the name of that bloody scribal boy was Ben Jones.*

So Hemmindale began his life as a farmer, and I began my miserable life as a Scribe. I enjoyed the fineries of that life, but every time I was alone, I would remember who I truly was. A poor beggar who'd made it into scribal school by chance—back when they'd allowed anyone to be tested, not just the wealthy. Obviously, that has changed.

When I saw Hemmindale again, he had married a woman from Blakenberge and was happy. I told him I would start giving him business if he could produce fresh fruit, and he offered me a peach. He doesn't remember his days with Marlowe and I, but I do. Recently, right after I met you, I saw him again. He comes to the theatre once every few months to honor his late wife. She loved the theatre and expensive things. But he couldn't leave Blakenberge for the sake of remembering his wife. It was bittersweet to see him living the life I was supposed to live. I was happy I wasn't poor; but I wasn't happy with the way I'd reached my false scribal status. Nonetheless, we began a new friendship as adults, and I would offer him my business for the scribal school when I could, without Marlowe knowing, of course.

I came back to the scribal house that fateful day long ago and told

Marlowe what'd happened. He didn't seem to care, until I threatened him. The only threat I had was me. I could come forth and tell everyone the truth of what happened that day, and if nothing else, the scribal school had records of who Ben Jones really was—and Hemmindale, too. It would be enough proof against Marlowe to have him put away or killed. I was hurt, Amana, I stood by and watched my only friend get beaten. But I guess much never changed about me. Once a coward, always a coward.

I let two more people slip through my hands, and the entire scribal program was halted until you came along.

As a desperate attempt to keep himself as the only Scribe, Marlowe took over the scribal program and pulled it to a stop when the president of the scribal school passed. Children stopped being tested; they were just sent there for school. He deemed it an opportunity for the elect to have a chance at private studies, while his pockets fattened from tuition payments. That's why you couldn't get in the day we met, because Marlowe wanted no succession. He didn't even like it when I called myself a Scribe.

The two other people I mentioned were women, just like you. They were sisters, twins actually. They both had the Gift. I found that out because I married one of them. When we finally married, my wife wanted to have no more secrets, so she told me she had the Gift. She and her sister knew things that were impossible to know unless you were Gifted. They could read a language and transcribe it so fluently; they were better than Hemmindale. I was amazed. They asked me if I could get them into the scribal house. I told them I couldn't and that should have been the end of it. But my wife, she was certainly like you. She didn't give up, and she knew she had to do something. So she met with Marlowe one day to explain that she and her sister weren't witches, but Marlowe didn't believe her. She told him to ask me, and when he did, I lied... ***again****.*

I told him this was the first time she'd ever spoken that way. I told him it was nonsense that a woman could become a Scribe, that it was just impossible. But Marlowe wasn't convinced. So he sent us to the courts. And the courts decided there was only one way to prove my innocence, and that was to light the fire of the stake my wife was tied to.

I did it, without a single tear. And I stoned her sister ... alone.

They wouldn't allow anyone else to throw stones, only me. That's why I hate myself. But you gave me hope, Amana. Even when I was mean you were kind. When I was so cruel and kept you there, you worked hard, even after you found out that it was a trap. I found that I wouldn't be able to live if you died never becoming a Scribe. I just hope I wasn't too late in realizing this.

It was silly, such kindness. Like the kind you only read about in books or in the Bible. I long to be with you, even if not as your trainer, just merely a friend, or maybe even more than that. I wanted you to find your happiness, to do what I kept everyone in my life from doing: becoming a real Scribe.

So, I've left you a key to my house out west. It's quiet and there are no neighbors, just a single house for miles. Everything you could need is there, except for mailing and printing. Start your career there, Amana, and become someone more than I have allowed you to be.

I want you to be free, and I know you will achieve that freedom.

In the bag, along with money and supplies, you'll find a script I left you. It's the best one Marlowe has ever written. Put your name on it and release it as your own. On the back of this note is the address to send it to and the house address. The people at the script address are in close relations with the Vatican council and the Jewish headquarters. These people will get you the acknowledgement you need. It may be hard as Favian, so you may want to come out as Shakespeare first.

No matter, I want to be clear, you have everything you need, Amana. You are the Scribe this world needs, and your writing is far superior to all of the Scribes who have come before you. So please, remember this, if nothing else,

You are ready.

X. Hemmindale (Ben)

Chapter Thirteen
Awakening

The words of Ben's letter stung. It hurt so bad to *read* the truth rather than hear it. I didn't know Ben had been a good man, I didn't know Ben at all. He was the pesky assistant that was plotting with Marlowe. That's all he'd been to me, but to him, I was so much more than what I thought I was to him.

Pain swelled in my chest. It made me ache day in and day out, and it made me drown in my tears every night. It became hard to write after I sent off Hamlet. I didn't want to write. I didn't even want to be a Scribe anymore. But what good would that do if Ben gave his life so that I could really become one? At the same time ... How could I go on?

I guess it hurt so much because I had been too dumb and too late to realize how much Ben had truly cared. I was so consumed with beating Marlowe, I didn't think about anything else. While Marlowe had definitively been my biggest roadblock, I wasn't becoming a Scribe to beat him, I was supposed to become a Scribe to do the will of God. But I lost track of that goal somehow.

When I told Ray I didn't know how to write anymore, he told me we should start heading west so I could discover the Gift again. So, one month after I read Ben's letter, Ray and I married and traveled out west. I kissed Ma goodbye and thanked her for her newfound kindness. I showed her gratitude for saving me. I hugged Pa tightly because we had lost so much time together, but I cherished the time we'd gained back. The distance would be hard on my parents, but they believed in me, and I held that deep in my heart. I promised them I would return and take care of them. But until I could return, I'd left them a sack of gold. I'd obtained so many gold callios from the time I'd stolen them from the Scribal house, the callios Ben left me, and the payments from the churches. Ray and I tried counting them, but the number was higher than 3,000, and Ray struggled to count past thirty and I was too tired to keep counting alone.

We'd converted some gold to paper as it would've been too heavy to carry them all. We also left some for Ray's family, as a goodbye gift and a way to get rid of the heavy coins. Ray left the sack of gold for his family on the ground with a note outside their shack. He decided not to see his family, he said it would be too hard to say goodbye again. When we left, I decided that I would rediscover the Gift to bring God glory.

"So, what are you going to do about that play Ben left you?" Ray asked. We'd finally gotten a carriage since Ben left me nearly every gold coin from the scribal house, plus all the other gold callios. Our carriage had an open top, but I placed an umbrella between the seats as shade from the sun. It was very comfortable, with plush red seats and a basket attached to the back to carry all our clothes. I rode in it the most, Ray didn't really like the carriage, he said it wasn't manly.

"I'm not stealing another thing if that's what you're asking." I wanted to cross my arms and get angry, but I knew Ray didn't mean what he asked in a negative way, I just felt annoyed because I was still embarrassed. All my thievery had brought so far was death.

"I didn't mean it like that." Ray had to speak loudly since his back was turned. Some days, I'd ride beside him on my horse, and he wouldn't have to shout. But I'd been wondering about that play all day. I wanted to sit comfortably so I could think.

"What do you think I should do with it?" Ray pulled the horses to a halt and hopped down. He would do this sometimes when he couldn't hear me very well.

"I think," Ray said as he stepped into the carriage. "I think you should put Marlowe's name on it. It might buy some time before people get suspicious about where he's been."

"True, but what if they start writing letters and wanting to meet with him? Then what?"

"I hadn't thought about that," Ray confessed.

We sat together in the carriage, still and quiet. I enjoyed moments like this with Ray. His arms securely around me, braving the coolness of the chilly evenings that quickly turned to cold nights.

"Ray?"

"Yeah?"

"Let's hold onto it for a while. Then maybe we can come up with another plan."

"Alright," Ray answered. He squeezed me tight and kissed my forehead. We'd been traveling for two weeks now and were finally nearing the west. We had to travel far from Blakenberge, but Ray and I believed it would be worth it.

The next day, we left our inn early. We were close enough to the new house that if we rode all day, we'd arrive at our new home by evening. It was Ray's idea to get us to the new house as soon as possible. He believed I'd have some kind of spiritual reawakening. It seemed, however, this spiritual reawakening was happening every day.

The long hours I'd sit in the carriage, or the times I'd ride my horse while Ray rested, I would speak with God. Talk with Him about all that was happening. He was quiet most days, but His reassuring voice and presence was always there when I needed it. I learned a bit more about God. How the subtle silences meant more than a definite answer. The way He would direct my thinking so that I could think the way He does. He would use instances and circumstances as examples to me and would often leave my thoughts swirling in my head, allowing me to learn to trust Him and listen for His voice.

I would ask Him silly questions, and it felt like I could feel His laughter, as radiant as the sun itself. He was so warm, so earnest, so pure. I spent most of those two weeks in outward silence, but inwardly, there was an ongoing conversation. Not only was I learning to trust God, but I was learning that God trusted me. He wasn't angry at me, not about Ben, or the plays I'd stolen, not even about Marlowe. He was only concerned for me, wanted me to be at my best, so we could work together. I found myself really falling in love with God, and it felt good, very good. Because God had forgiven me before I'd ever forgiven myself. I wasn't perfect, but neither were any of the folks from the Bible —except Jesus, of course. I wasn't beyond redemption, in fact, I had already been redeemed by Christ at Calvary. Now it was time to walk in that redemption. No more lying, no more stealing, no more shooting folks; not even the bad folks.

"Amana?" I heard Ray calling to me as I drifted back to consciousness.

"Yes?" I surrendered to a long stretch before Ray could speak. I could feel the carriage slowing as he said, "Amana, we've made it."

I was ecstatic. I nearly jumped from the carriage, ready to see this house. I imagined it would be old and small, but to my surprise, it was not. It was old but it had a modern look to it. And it was nothing short of a castle. Windows all over the brick building. It sat so far away from the road; the windows looked small from a distance. When we got close, I could see the wonderful design of the place. It was a home fit for the richest, which made sense considering when Ben acquired this property, he was a "Scribe."

"I can't believe there are houses this big!" I said as Ray helped me from the carriage. He didn't say anything, just stood in awe for a moment before he smiled and nodded, momentarily lost for words.

It was beautiful. The green grass gave way to an immaculate pavement that led you to the side of the house, where a big white door sat glistening.

"Let's check out the inside," I said to Ray, eyeing that door.

We held hands as we made our way over, but before we could reach for the handle, the door opened, and we were greeted by a fleet of servants. They wore black and white, men and women of different ages and races.

A tall dark man stepped forward from the fleet and said, "Welcome. You must be Favian." The man extended a hand to me. I placed mine in his and he kissed it. "We've been waiting for you, ma'am. Ben left us detailed instructions of your care. He did not mention that someone would be joining you, however." His eyes slid over to Ray, expressionless—neither impressed nor unimpressed. Just staring, like he was waiting for an explanation.

I was lost for words, but a sudden jab from Ray made me speak, "Uh, yes! This is my husband, Murray Castillo. We just got married a few weeks ago, so Ben never got the chance to meet him."

The room was silent, and we all shifted uncomfortably. But the man regained his composure before I did. "Well, Favian, Murray, welcome to your humble estate. Ben has informed us that you are a Scribe, Mrs. Favian, and he expects us to be at your every command. Your main focus here is to enjoy your life in perfect relaxation and peace so that you may write and read as much as you desire. We will take care of the rest. There will never be a need to leave this house; however, you are free to do as you please. I'll have my men take your luggage while I give you a small tour." I only nodded, still absolutely amazed, as our things were swept from us and carried away.

"Please follow me," the man said.

Ray gripped my hand, and we started our tour.

"As you know, Ben was not a Scribe. But he was upheld as one, since there were no other Scribes, until now, of course. So, as Ben was deemed a Scribe, he deemed me his assistant, even though the program had been dismissed. Ben and I were friends in the scribal school. But when he left, I didn't see him again until much later." We walked through the house as the man spoke; his voice was elegant, as smooth as melted chocolate. He could have talked me to sleep, and I would have been just as happy.

Ben's assistant described his days with Ben as fun; he even told us how Ben asked him to look over the estate here. Not only was the house beautiful, but there was a fully functioning farm right on our property, and there were maids and butlers at our service whenever we needed. I would never have to lift a finger as long as I was here. When the tour neared its end, the man stopped us before two large double doors.

"Behind these doors is something Ben left just for you, Favian. You may enter as you please, and you will find great use for the key Ben left you. You two are like royalty here. So please don't hesitate to ring your bell for us to meet you wherever you are. We want to honor Ben's final wish, and honor you as a Gifted one. So, this is the end of the tour. Your room is right down the hall; Ben had us fill your wardrobe already, but early tomorrow we will take Murray's measurements and start a wardrobe for him as well." He placed a hand over his chest and nodded at us.

As he turned to leave, I said, "Excuse me! What is your name?"

"Call me, Black," he replied, voice like a song echoing off the high walls.

I nodded and watched Black walk down the long hall. I turned to Ray and said, "I don't think I'm ready to see what's behind these doors yet."

"Well, let's go to our room, then," Ray said.

Our first night was sleepless. Giggles and warmth filled the room until dawn. Ray and I had never indulged in one another. The moment never seemed right, but for some reason it did during that night. A loud knock came at the door, but Ray nor I answered. A few moments later another knock came, and from beneath a tangle of blankets, I called, "Come in!" I heard the doors open as I wrapped myself in the silk covers.

"Good morning, Mr. and Mrs. Favian. We are here to

bathe and attend to you. We will also be taking Mr. Favian's measurements."

"I'm sorry, Favian is my name, my *first* name. You must mean Mr. and Mrs. *Castillo*."

"I'm very sorry, malady, but we must honor the Gifted one."

I looked over at Ray who didn't seem to care either way. He was beaming like a star, and I tried not to feel embarrassed.

"Ok, please prepare a bath for us."

"Would you like one together or separate?"

"Separate"

"Together!"

I looked at Ray, but he was just smiling with his stupid face. I rolled my eyes and said, "Together."

The maids smiled wide and let a gentle giggle escape between the two of them. I sighed, hoping that the air I pushed out would push away the embarrassment. The maids curtseyed and sashayed out of the room.

"Man! This feels good! Isn't this what we always wanted, Amana?" Ray wiggled beneath the blankets and reached up to play with my hair. It'd grown out more, cascading down to my waist. "A fancy place, with fancy clothes, and people doing all the hard work for us? Remember that?" He pulled me back into an embrace and I laid there soaking in the moment. His bare skin pressed against mine; I traced my finger over the nearly completely healed wound on his chest.

"I do remember, Ray. It just doesn't seem real. I'm still trying to believe it all. I'm still trying to cope with the fact that Ben had to die to leave this all to me and—"

"Amana, stop going back there. It was so hard to dig you out of that hole. I don't want to see you like that again."

I sighed. He was right. The month before we left, I'd spent so much time moping around and crying about Ben. But Ray was there, and he really did help me out of the dark hole I'd sank into.

"I'm sorry, Ray."

He kissed my head, and then grabbed a handful of my loose hair. "I never knew your hair was this long. You braid was long, but I think it looks longer when its loose." He smelled my hair for a moment. "I love you so much."

"I love you too, Ray."

The bath was delightful. We enjoyed every moment in ways I can't describe, then we cleaned up once the maids returned. It was beautiful. A tub so wide Ray and I both fit comfortably, with hot water poured in from the maids. The floor was perfect marble, swirling with its natural, God-given design, and the walls were painted in a mural by an artist I couldn't name. There was a window with an astonishing view of the rolling hills outside, when I wasn't peering out, I was enjoying the sunlight that washed in through the open curtains.

After the bath, I left for the room with the double doors while Ray got his measurements taken. I followed the long marble hallway covered in a grey carpet. I looked at the great craftsmanship and intricate designs of the walls. There were paintings of fruit and marketplaces hanging. Ben seemed to have an odd taste in art, but I enjoyed getting to see what he'd liked. It was a reflection of his time in Blakenberge. At the scribal house, it wasn't about Ben, it was all about me and Marlowe, so I never really found out much about him.

The hall was long, but when I finally reached the doors, I was surprised to find them unlocked. As I pushed open the door, a whiff of old paper filled my nose. There were shelves stacked onto each other, all filled with books. There was a desk in the center with a grand chair, carved from fine wood, it looked as lavish as the house itself. On the desk were papers scattered around. The floor was covered in piles of books and papers. I was afraid to walk in.

The room smelled of responsibility and awakening. I knew once I stepped through that door, I would have an overwhelming conviction to fulfill some duty, but there would be a great awakening within me.

I stepped forward, letting the double doors close behind me. I took careful steps through the room, missing the piles of books and stepping over loose pieces of paper. All the words on the papers were in various languages. All of which I understood, but something was different; there was nothing written in English. I picked up some of the papers from the cool floor. Some were so old they were brittle in my fingers, while others were fresher pages, but still held a thick layer of dust. I opened a book sitting atop a neat pile that stacked from the floor to my waist. It was a book of geography; there were maps and coordinates inside. I flicked through the pages when something gold caught my eye. I looked up from the book and saw Ben's gold pocket watch sitting on a folded piece of paper.

My heart sank as I stared at the watch. It took me back to the time when I first met Ben. I wanted to break down and sob, but I managed to pick up the watch and stare at it. There was a bold insignia carved into the gold: it was a figure-eight. When I clicked on the small button, the watch opened and revealed an inscription in Croatian.

Time is infinite, you are not.

A small tear ran down my cheek and I found myself chuckling at the inscription.

"Ok, Ben, I'll get to work," I whispered.

I sat down at the desk and opened the folded paper to read it aloud.

"Dear Amana, I know you must have grown tired of hearing from me by now. Another call from the grave, I suppose. Well, this is the final one. Do you remember the story I left you by Marlowe and the place I told you to send it to? Well, that place is extremely important. If your work on this piece is good, they'll work with you through the distance, but if it's *very* good, they'll expect to meet with you in person. They'll invite you to an event to show everyone your excellent writing. That will be up to you to decide if you're ready to announce to the world who you really are. But if you decide to go, don't go emptyhanded.

"You will be in the presence of royalty, King James and his accompaniment visiting from across the seas (he usually visits for something like this). He'll be expecting a gift, so I've left you one last task; give him something more valuable than anything else. That is something I know you'll be able to understand. I'll be the first to say it, Amana, congratulations on becoming the first female Scribe to be recognized. But I also want to thank you for going through great lengths to *become* the first female Scribe recognized.

"Do well, Amana, you don't need anyone looking over your work anymore. You are ready."

The words renewed me while engulfing me in an unbearable sadness. My chest ached for Ben, but I didn't want to miss him again. I sat with my head on the desk, thinking about the two letters from him. He was specific about reworking the play from Marlowe, but I knew he wanted me to write my own work. He didn't know if I was confident enough in myself to write my own stories, but I appreciated Ben's kind gesture. I knew I'd have to come up with something to blow the crowd away when I revealed the Gift to any of the royals I might run into. I told myself to think of that later. For now, I needed to focus on what I could write of my own that would get me an invitation. Could I even write something that good? I began to doubt myself when I suddenly felt a warmth rush up my spine, and the voice of the Spirit of God (the Holy Spirit) said to me,

You have been crafted in the image of God. Do not doubt who God has called you to be.

I nodded my head in agreement. I could feel the traces of doubt leaving and my mind clearing. "Ok, God, give me something to write about, then."

I held my face in my hands as I prayed aloud. Silence. I listened hard for the Voice of God, and I heard Him say in the quiet of my heart ...

Marlowe.

"Marlowe? What kind of story could I write about Marlowe?"

I paused and thought about all that Ben had explained in the first letter. The way Marlowe would do anything for power, and the way he never wanted a successor. I could feel a story being poured into me. I reached for a pen and began to write.

"I will call Marlowe, Macbeth."

Chapter Fourteen
The Day Shakespeare Died

As I lay in bed with Ray, I remembered where I found the second letter from Ben. I never unlocked whatever it was he'd had for me. Ray and I were enjoying our lives here at our new home. When we first arrived, he would often lounge around while I worked in the den. Sometimes he would visit me, sometimes I would read him stories while he ate. Ray loved adventure stories the most. He liked to imagine the faraway places and distant lands. Sometimes we'd spend hours in the den, me reading and Ray listening. It was a pleasant way to pass time, but after a while, Ray began to feel, "small."

One day he came to visit me in the den and said, "What do you think about me getting a job?"

I looked up at him from my stack of papers. He was loudly munching on an apple. "I think that's ridiculous," I laughed. "What else would we need the money for?"

"It's not about money, Amana." His tone was suddenly dark, like he was annoyed.

I set my pen down and sighed. "What's wrong, Ray? Why do you want a job now?"

He sucked his teeth and started pacing the room, still munching on that apple. He hated when I asked him about things directly. Even though Ray had matured quite a bit during our time apart, it was times like this that reminded me he was still that shy kid selling goods in the market for his family. That timid, awkward part of him still existed somewhere inside, preferring me to use the context clues of our conversation to understand him—instead of saying what was wrong outright.

It wasn't that I had a problem with working around Ray's shyness, it was that he wasn't saying much for me to draw clues from, so I had to ask him straight up. We stared at each other for a moment, neither of us speaking, just looking and wondering—trying to figure out what the other was thinking. Then Ray took another bite of his apple, still refusing to speak. With a sigh, I went back to writing. He would tell me when he was ready.

Ray took his time, munching, swallowing, and sighing. He repeated the actions until the apple was gone, all while

I worked quietly, putting finishing touches on 'Macbeth.' Another sigh and finally Ray said, "I'm embarrassed."

This is a start, I thought, giving him an encouraging nod.

"You're always working and I'm always just here," he huffed. "When we were at the market, we both worked, but I felt like I could take care of you if I had to. Now," he paused, "you take care of me."

My head snapped up; he was staring right at me. Sad eyes and a downturned mouth, it was a side of Ray I'd never seen before. He was so vulnerable, so open. I moved from my desk across the den to him. "Ray," I said grabbing his hands, it was awkward at first because he was still holding the core to his apple, but he threw it away and then clasped my hands just fine. "I work because I have to," I said. "It's a privilege not to have to work. Aren't you proud of me?"

He cupped my face and winced. But not in pain, it was out of disappointment. "I'm so proud of you, Amana, more than you could ever imagine. But I still want to take care of you. I'm your husband; I want to be a man and provide for my wife—not lay around all day."

I tried to protest but he hushed me with a shake of his head. "You're the one working hard and I'm just here enjoying the fruits of your labor. I can't stand it anymore." His hands dropped from my face, but I caught them in mine.

I understood how he felt. Men in our town were raised to protect and provide for a household. But since Ben left everything to me, and now I was Shakespeare, *and* a Scribe, Ray felt like he didn't fit in. But I knew how he felt. Besides the way we'd been raised, I knew the feeling of wanting to rescue someone who didn't need rescuing. Having that desire to help someone who didn't need it left you feeling empty and lonely.

"Ray, you do more for me than you understand," I said softly. "I love when you come to visit me in the den, and I love that you're always right there as soon as I leave. You're my one and only support system here. All we have is each other. My parents, Black, and the others support me, but our folks are miles away and Black is just following Ben's last orders. You're the one who's right here beside me. I need you to be here, Ray. That's the job you have now."

Slowly, he pulled his hands away and said harshly, "That's not enough." The conversation shifted as his bitter words filled the air. "Ben took care of you, and I saw you cry countless nights over him. You shed tears for another man who took care of you and is *still* taking care of you even from the grave! And all I have to offer is *support*? I wonder; if I die, would you weep for me the way you did for him?"

The air was cold and stale. I adjusted, shifting my

weight from one foot to the other. "That was mean, Ray. I have loved you with everything in me. Ben died for two reasons; because I was foolish enough to steal someone's work and think there would be no consequences. And the other reason? Because I left to find you again. If I never would've left that house, Marlowe would've found me and killed *me*, not Ben." I glared at him, hating him for building this wall between us. I never wanted to tell him these things—never wanted to think about Ben's death again, but here I was, reliving those horrible moments all over again because Ray's ego had been bruised.

It wasn't my fault I had the Gift. It wasn't my fault God gave me a job to do and I was willing to obey and do it. Ray had no right to go bringing up Ben like this—comparing himself to a man whose grave was still fresh. I balled my hands into fists as I said, "The only reason Ben's dead body is still rotting in that scribal house is because I left him to save you. Every time I've had a choice, I picked you. Romeo and Juliet was written because I realize I would die if you died. But only *your* feelings matter now, right?" He tried to speak but it was my time to hush him now with a shake of my head. "After all I did for you—for *us*. When we arrived here, they expected me to come alone. But I brought you here and assured them you were with me. Ray, I *married* you. I agreed to spend the rest of my life— every single day that I live—with you. How could you think that about me?"

He ran his hands through his hair and pouted. "I'm just angry."

"But why?"

"Because I wish I could've done more for you."

Silence again.

"You went through a lot, and you have all these connections with all these people I don't know. You know how to be fancy, and you know a lot about all of the fancy foods they feed us here. But I'm just a poor market hustler, living it good off his wife's fortune. I'm just so jealous and angry. I'm hurt." He turned away from me, like he didn't want me to watch him issue his confession. "I wish I could've been who Ben was to you. I wish *I* could've made our lives better. I wish I wasn't poor and had no mannerisms. I wish ... I wish you were like the old Amana. When you only *dreamed* of being a Scribe." He sighed. "You haven't changed, but our situation has, and I feel left behind. Like I still need to catch up but there's no way I can. We're too far apart."

I knew this conversation would come, but it hurt more than I'd expected. I tried to stay levelheaded so he wouldn't feel any smaller than he was. With strength I didn't know I had, I exhaled my anger and did what I've always done. I put Ray first. Because we weren't just kids with big dreams anymore. We were adults who were married and living in reality. This problem wasn't going to fix itself, this wall between us wouldn't come down until one of us started removing the bricks. That one would be me. But I couldn't take credit away from Ray; he'd tried, in his own awkward way. He'd sat down and thought up what he thought was a solution—getting a job—and he'd tried to bring it up to me, but that just dissolved into an argument.

We could still fix this if we wanted to.

I took a deep breath. "Ray, you are exactly who I need you to be. I don't need another Ben Jones in my life. I don't need a fancy husband or someone super extravagant. That's the best part of you, Ray. I can be myself with you. I can be old Amana again, the girl who aspired to become a Scribe, who wondered about the fancy life and what it would be like. I can be the girl in the market who stood just one tent over trying to make a sell. We have so much in common, yet you're forgetting we both started in the same place." I smiled, even though part of me wanted to cry. "You keep looking around at who we are here, but remember where we came from, *together*. If I needed someone else, Ray, I wouldn't have married you. You want to provide for me? Continue listening to the stories I read you. Curl up with me at the end of the day. Kiss my head like you do every time you leave the den. I want everything you've been giving me. Why isn't that enough?"

He shrugged his shoulders, still turned around so I couldn't see his face. I sat on the floor and gathered my skirt around myself. "Come sit with me."

Slowly, Ray moved over to me and slid to the floor. I patted the area in front of me and he moved over. "Lean back." I massaged his shoulders as we sat in silence again. Ray picked up a book and stared at it.

"What's so great about these things anyways?" he mumbled.

Ray couldn't read. He was able to understand a bit, and he was better than his family, but other than some of the common language, Ray couldn't read much. Most books weren't written in the common language, because common people couldn't read. But I knew Ray's ability to *learn to read* was present, it just hadn't been nurtured. So I told him to open the book. He groaned but opened it anyway.

"When these two letters are together like that, they make a *'th'* sound. Try it."

He stared for a moment more and then said, "*Th*."

"Good! Do you know the alphabet and their sounds?"

He shook his head in my lap, and I told him, "Well, that's alright. We can do the alphabet tomorrow. Let's just start with this word." I pointed back to the letters and described the sounds to him. He echoed me and nodded as we sat there together. After an hour, Ray was exhausted.

Softly, he said to me, "I'm sorry, Amana. I said some things I shouldn't have. I feel bad when I see you working so hard, like I'm just a burden."

I smiled down at him. "You've met your first set of goals; you just need to set new ones. You dreamed of living lavish and eating good food. Since we've accomplished that, it's time to aspire to do something else."

"Like what?"

"Well, you like fruit," I said. "Maybe you can start a small apple orchard here. We've got plenty of land. I'm sure Black wouldn't mind getting a team together to help you. And once your apples are growing, maybe you can ride into town and sell them to bakers and eateries. You could even give them away. We've got a whole farm to ourselves; we don't need all this stuff. Maybe we can give back a little. Help out people still living in poverty."

Ray thought for a moment. "It could be like selling in the market back in Blankenberge."

I nodded, smoothing out his hair. "You could start a foundation. Help feed all those hungry kids and other folk. Our farm could do some good in this world."

He let out a sigh, like he was finally letting go of all his anger and all those feelings of uselessness. "Ok," he said. "I'll start tomorrow ... Thank you, Amana."

I leaned over and this time I kissed *his* head. "You're welcome."

* * *

The next morning, Ray left the bed before me and headed straight to Black to discuss his orchard idea. I took my time getting ready, all the while thinking about what I should get as a gift if I'm invited to a function. This had been swirling in the back of my head since I began writing "Macbeth." I was able to push it away while I worked on the play, but since I finished it and sent it off early this morning (by way of the maids), a gift was the only thing left to come up with.

"Maybe Ben has already left me something I can give to the king," I said as I sat in the den. Quickly, I got to my feet and started searching for a keyhole. I looked on the shelves, the desk, the paneling, until I found a small keyhole on the fullest shelf in the room.

I held the key that Ben left me and kissed it. *Click. Click.* Suddenly the large shelf began to move, and the double doors locked. I ran to the doors and shook the handles.

"I'm locked in!" I shouted as I pounded on the door. But no one answered. Finally, the shelf stopped sliding and gave way to a small hallway. On the wall leading down the hall was a torch. I lit it using supplies from the shelves back in the den and started down the hall.

"Hello?" I called into the darkness.

My bare feet felt cold on the concrete floor. I traced my free hand against the wall, feeling all the bricks. Cool air chilled me as I continued. At the end of the hall was a door with a sign that read "Push." I pushed the door, and when it opened, the torch blew out. But I didn't need the torch. Diamonds glistened from within the walls, blinding me. The floor was made of marble, and the single circular pillar was, too. The walls were marbled with diamonds embedded in them, and a small window gave way for the sun to shine brightly into the white room. In the center of the room was a small white display. A book sat open on a beautiful glimmering stump. There was a glass encasing over the book. The pages looked frail, but the words were written so beautifully. As I got closer, I was able to recognize the language the book was written in, Greek. *Such a fine language*, I thought.

"The book of the generation of Jesus Christ, the son of David, the son of Abraham," I read aloud. I blinked twice before I realized what I was reading. I covered my mouth as tears trickled down my cheeks. My hands trembled as I reached for the glass container. Gently, I removed the glass and set it on the floor. I placed my hand on the Words and breathed deeply. I flipped one page back and found the text was written in Hebrew. Beneath the book was a small sheet of paper sticking out. I pulled it softly from under the book and recognized Ben's handwriting.

If you've made it this far, then you know my secret, that I am not really a Scribe. Therefore, I could not read this, but you who found this can. I paid a hefty price to get this Book, the first bound Bible. Only remove the glass for short moments at a time and never remove the Word from this room.
Take care of it, be blessed.

In that moment, I knew what my calling was. I discovered what God had been wanting me to do for a very long time, and I knew then what gift would be suitable for a king.

That was the day Shakespeare died.

Chapter Fifteen
My Name is Favian Amana Hart

Scribes are special people with a special purpose. We have been given a gift that allows us to understand foreign languages without ever hearing it beforehand, read without ever being taught, speak with fluidity, and write cohesively. We are the very elect who are bestowed with the trust of God to bring His light to His people.

The scribal program began back in Biblical times. Many men were deemed as Scribes, but they weren't as gifted as the next generation, or the generation of Scribes after that. They weren't even as gifted as me. Every time a Scribe is born, God bestows more trust and more honor unto that person, and we carry the torch for His people. While Marlowe nearly ruined this blessing, I have been chosen to breathe life back into it. Get the Gift and the program back on the course it needs to be for men *and* women.

The scribal program never intended for women *not* to be Scribes but after so long with not a single woman being recognized as such, many thought the female sex simply wasn't able to be Gifted. When they tried to come forth, the courts had those women killed for blasphemy. But God did not want another woman killed, so He raised me up to follow the path He'd planned for me in advance.

Although I got a little lost becoming Shakespeare and trying to prove myself, when I found the original Biblical text, a fire within me was kindled. God revealed to me that Scribes were meant to translate and correct the language— not rewrite or change history. Our duties were only to further the spread of the Gospel, never to decide who is privy to it and who is not. So I have decided I will no longer be that way.

I will write no more plays as Shakespeare, and I will no longer work hard for myself. Now, I will work for the Kingdom of God.

When I told this to Ray, he was happy—so happy he actually cried and told me I had his support. As we ate our dinner, Black ran in from the rain. "Mrs. Favian, it has arrived."

I looked at the sealed scroll he held in his hand and knew it was from the king. Ray glanced over at me with big, curious eyes.

I tried to calm myself. "Bring it to me."

Black calmly strolled across the dining hall, dripping wet from the rain. Each footstep made my heart pound louder and faster. Finally, he handed me the scroll. It had a crimson ribbon tied over it, traced in silver. The material felt nice in my hand as I gently tugged the ribbon loose. *This is it*, I thought, taking a big breath. This was the moment I'd been hoping would come.

I unrolled the scroll and felt the room shift with tension and anxiety. Ray leaned closer, even Black peered over, briefly forgetting his normally poised demeanor.

I read aloud, "Dear Shakespeare, I am writing to you personally, with my own hand and pen, to tell you that your work is profound. It is a work of complex beauty and intricacies that even the wisest could not produce. You have such a way with the pen, making every stroke mean something more than ink on a page. You are quite fine at your work, fine indeed. Thus, I am extending an invitation to you.

"I want you and your entourage to join me at a feast being held in my honor. I will have fine dining and beautiful music, poetry that I'm sure won't outshine your own. I wish to honor you at a celebration meant to honor me. I want to give your work my seal so that all the land will know it is I who have deemed this work an intellectual property. This will also allow you to enter the scribal house with no opposition. Accept my invitation, if you would.

"The feast will be in three days. For honor and prestige, King James."

There was a moment of silence before the room burst into enormous sound. Cheers and hugs. We were excited to be recognized and invited by the king, it was everything I could have wanted.

I watched the cheering go on. Ray smiled and talked loudly as a fleet of servants filled the hall, drawn in by our celebration. The cooks emerged from the kitchen, even those who'd been in the fields somehow heard the excitement and joined us. I watched the wave of joy wash over the small sea of people. I hadn't been the only one hoping for this, I realized. All of these people had been hoping—possibly since Ben gathered them all here. I was finally able to take a step that would mean something. *Ben, I did it*, I said quietly within.

We spent the next three days getting things together. Black ordered us a new carriage, the maids bathed me in perfumes and oils, combing my hair, prepping my skin for the big day. Our chefs gave us celebratory meals every night, and the farmers harvested the best fruit of the season. Meanwhile, Ray tried to keep busy. He stayed in his new apple orchard most of the time. I could tell he was nervous and excited. He didn't ask about my plans for the feast or the gift, either. His nervous glances and tense silence told me all I needed to know. He was more anxious than I was, which was understandable. Ray hadn't experienced a lot outside of Blakenberge until recently with me. From his kind smile, and his quasi-brave attitude, to the supportive words he kept throwing at me, Ray was growing more unnerved every day.

The morning of the event, Ray and I stayed in bed a bit longer. Our lovely assistants stayed away for a while, while Ray and I slept in. We lay there in bed with the silk sheets engulfing us in the waves of blue fabric. Recently, it'd been too warm for the blanket, so we just slept under the sheets. I listened to Ray's breathing, steady, deep, clear. His chest rose and fell against my skin as he held me close. His warm breath danced over my neck, tickling every hair. His arm, once small and slender, lay across me, now heavy and muscular. My deep brown hand rested atop his honey-toned hand. We looked like peanut butter and chocolate swirled together.

As I lay there, I knew tonight would change our lives forever, and every word, glance, and nonverbal signal would mean something for more than just me. It would mean something for God's Kingdom, the scribal program, my husband, and our fleet of workers, my parents, all of Blakenberge, for Ben and Hemmindale, too. Tonight was not about me. I was just the figurehead. Tonight would be about all the things I stood for and the changes that only I would be able to make, God willing.

"Good morning, Mrs. Castillo." Ray hardly ever called me by our last name. He still referred to me as Hart, I think he wasn't used to the name change yet. But today, he just wanted to step out of his comfort zone since he knew we would be thrown into a new world, whether for good or bad, by the end of the night.

"Good morning, Mr. Castillo. What are your plans today?" I returned.

Ray squeezed me tight and nuzzled my head with his. "I'm going to check on the orchard, of course."

I loved Ray because he knew me so well. Above everything else, I wanted today to function like a normal day, nothing special until the evening. I enjoyed my time here, but with the night approaching, I wanted to cherish the little things that might change.

"Good," I said, smiling. "I'll come visit, since I don't plan to spend very long in my den."

"Really?" He perked up. "I'd love for you to come see, but the trees are small—mostly just plots of seeds. We only found a few trees from a nearby orchard who had babies to spare."

I bunched my shoulders. "Actually, I expected it to just be piles of dirt." We laughed for a moment, then sat in silence. I fiddled with the blankets, all kicked to the side of the bed.

"Have you decided on a gift yet?" Ray asked, almost shyly.

I quirked an eyebrow. "Kind of late to ask."

"I wanted to leave it totally up to you. So I didn't say anything," he explained. "But I've been dying to know what you selected."

I sighed. "I'm not even sure if he'll like it, but I'm waiting to reveal it at the feast."

Ray stretched and rolled over; he laid flat out in the bed and stared up at the ceiling. "I know it'll be great."

"I'll call the maids so we can get ready for the day." I rolled onto Ray and kissed him.

After breakfast, Ray went out to his orchard, and I went to the den. I sat at my desk reading through some of the shorter books, wasting time. I loved the way the pages sounded when they turned, the rustling noise brought excitement and wonder with just a simple turn. I looked for that sound in books. Not every page turned the same way. Some had louder rustling, some with thinner, finer paper made a soft rustling noise. Those heavy with ink made more of a windy noise, but I enjoyed listening to the pages. Every single one. It was a noise all too familiar for me, and one I would always cherish.

As I sat in the den reading, I finally decided to ring the

bell for Black. It would take him a moment to reach me, so I began to clean up my work. I traced over the pile of scripts I had. Every play I'd ever written, even the ones I stole from Marlowe. I felt a sullen sadness as I loomed over the works. I'd poured my all into them, but I knew it was time to walk away. I reminded myself the Bible tells us there's a season for everything, and that when we grow up, we put away childish things. While my scripts weren't the least bit childish, I knew that Shakespeare was dead. He'd served his purpose for a very long time, but now, it was time to move on. As I wrapped the scripts in paper, I heard a knock on the door.

"Come in."

Black entered the room and came to the desk. "You rang, Mrs. Favian."

"I did. Take this." I handed him a book as thick as a Bible and continued. "Have this prepared for tonight. I want a fine leather binding on here. I've left instructions, so you'll know what to do."

Black looked over the heavy book. He gaped at it for a moment and then nodded. "What a wonderful gift."

I nodded and he turned to leave, but I called out to him. "Oh, and Black?"

He spun to face me once more, eyebrows raised.

"Send my husband in, I'm ready to see his orchard now."

"Of course." He nodded and left for good this time.

I waited in the den, praying that God would give me favor and mercy tonight. As I closed my prayer and meditated on a Scripture in silence, Ray entered the den.

"Are you ready to see the apples now?" He greeted me with a smile, and I said, "Yes."

Taking me by the hand, Ray led me out to his grove.

I was stunned by the beauty. The small twigs sprung up from the dirt while mounds of dirt were lined up in rows. It was pleasant to take in and to imagine the amount of life and creation happening where our eyes couldn't see.

"It's lovely, Ray."

He smiled his goofy, handsome smile and chuckled. "I helped cultivate the ground a bit. So now I just come out here and check on them, prune whatever needs pruning." He shrugged. "It's not much right now, but once they begin to *really* grow, it'll be a lot of work."

"I'm so proud of you and your orchard. You did a great job."

Ray pulled me close. I knew there were a thousand things that could've been said in that moment, but a warm embrace from Ray was all I wanted.

* * *

The evening came and the house began to stir. The maids ran me a hot bath filled with more perfumes and oils than the other days. They'd been giving me perfumed baths so I would have an "impressive" fragrance. The oils aided in keeping the perfumes locked into my skin while also moisturizing me. Ray had mentioned the last two nights that I'd smelled "delicious and sweet."

I sat in the bath, relaxing in the peaceful quiet. I wanted to stay there, warm and light. But just as I was starting to prune, a maid entered and told me my room was ready. Little did I know, the room had been filled with clothes and face-paint.

I rested across the portable bed as the servant massaged me. Her small hands worked deftly, pushing down gently with delicate fingers and sometimes a strange, cool metal. I enjoyed the massage since it gave me something else to think about. In the quiet moments, I chose not to dwell on the evening. Right now, I just wanted to enjoy the quiet.

I heard the door open, and the maid shouted, "She's not dressed!"

"It's just me," Ray said.

"My apologies, sir," her voice faltered, afraid she would be admonished. "Should I finish, or would you like me to leave?"

"Stay." Ray walked around the bed and motioned toward me with an open palm. "Please continue."

Slowly, she went back to the massage.

"Have you picked out a gown yet?" Ray asked.

I closed my eyes and listened to his footsteps as he walked through the room, probably looking at all the clothes.

"Not yet. As you can see, there's plenty for me to choose from."

"There is," he chuckled lightly.

"Mrs. Favian, we are finished," the maid said. "We would like you to pick out a dress while I prepare the hair and paint team."

"Ok. I'll be ready in five minutes."

The woman laid a blanket over me and left the room.

"I have to go down to see Black. He's got some clothing for me to try," Ray said. He helped me wrap in the blanket and move from the stretcher. "What are you thinking about wearing?"

"Hmm," I mumbled, glancing through the wardrobe. Fancy fabrics, bright colors, and dark, neutral tones were displayed before me. All the material felt different, some itchy, some comfortable. I looked through the pieces, trying to ignore the wave of disappointed rolling over me. There wasn't anything I particularly liked. I was just about to pout when Ray walked up and pulled out a gown; a deep rouge dress that melted into faded black. It was stunning.

"I think you'd look great in this." He held it up for me

to see.

"I love it," I said, running my hands over the material. "I'll wear it."

Ray leaned over and kissed me just as a knock sounded at the door. "Come in," I called, pulling away. A troop of maids rushed inside, ready to work.

"Alright," I shrugged sheepishly, but Ray was already turning to leave.

"I'll see you at the gate, then," he said over his shoulder.

I watched him leave in silence. His nerves were getting to him; he was starting to shut down and close me out.

* * *

I was guided out the house and around to the front. I wore the dress Ray had picked out with face-paint so elegant, even I was impressed. Today the women did not wrap my hair. They left it loose to hang down my back. I did not protest at all; I wanted to do something special for this feast, and revealing my hair was personally satisfying.

Atop my head, I wore a headdress made of netted material. It came down over my forehead with black crosses dangling from the ends. The red corset was laced with black strings that led down to the rest of the dress. I wore a red fluffy shawl that made the gown explode with beauty and sass.

As I stepped out, I saw Ray. He wore all black. His jacket was short in the front with a long train in the back while the inside was red. He wore a top hat with a matching red trim, and his pants met the top of his red shoes. The cane in his hand was red and black, and black gloved hands held the cane.

We were drooling over each other for so long that Black finally said, "You both look stunning, but if we wait any longer, we'll be late."

Ray extended his hand, a goofy smile on his face; I took it and smiled just as stupidly as he helped me into the carriage. We rode in silence, with the anticipation so thick I felt like I would choke. By the time we arrived, my smile had melted into a grimace.

Ray grabbed my hand. "Are you ready?"

I breathed heavily. "Yes."

A very forced smile worked its way onto my lips as Black opened the carriage doors. The outside brimmed with music and lights. The people walking along the green pathways wore expensive clothes, loud jewelry, and tall wigs. Everyone looked so nice; for once, Ray and I fit right in.

I saw Ray ogling at everything and nudged him, but he just kept walking and staring with no shame. As we approached the building, a man in tights said, "Your name, please?"

I looked up at the bearded man and back at Black. Black nodded and said, "We are part of Shakespeare's entourage."

"And where is Shakespeare himself?"

"He'll be making a *grand* entrance soon enough."

The bearded man stared intensely at Black who was completely unfazed. Finally, he nodded and said, "Go in."

Once we got inside, I exhaled heavily. "Nice job, Black. I thought we were done back there."

Black let go of an uncharacteristically hearty laugh. "We've come too far. We were getting in today. No matter what."

I grabbed his hand and gave it a squeeze as thanks. He squeezed it back.

As we rounded the corner, we entered what I realized was the throne room. Sitting on a golden chair on an elevated dais was a man wearing a crown of wrought gold and encrusted with red and green jewels. His clothes were so extraordinary, I doubted paper money or even gold callios could afford them. Purples, golds, whites, blues. He was important, and I knew right away he was King James.

A smaller man ran up to him as we approached and whispered in his ear. He nodded a few times and then directed his attention to us. A smile stretched across his face as he said, "Welcome to my feast! I hear Shakespeare is waiting to make an entrance. That man is such a mystery.

But his work is wonderful."

I smiled back, all anxiety gone as I stepped forward and said loudly, "Thank you! I worked rather hard on every piece."

The king tilted his head, and the buzz around us began to hush. People were staring at us—at *me*—the same way they did when I'd entered the printing press of the Black owner all that time ago.

"Excuse me?" the king said. "Surely you mean *Shakespeare*—possibly your husband, or, rather, your master?"

I shook my head. "No. I mean me. This is Murray Castillo, my husband." Beside me, Ray smiled and offered a little wave. In that moment, I could have kissed him. His shameless country tendencies put me at ease.

"And who are you?" the king asked.

"Before I tell you that, I need to say something. Please, if you will lower the music." Interested, the king waved his hand and the music lowered.

"I'll amuse you, go ahead."

I looked at Ray; he was nervous but also somehow confident. I looked over at Black; he was smiling, holding my gift in his bag. I felt a calming sensation wash over me as I looked at them both. Ray gave me a nod, filling me with a sudden surge of surety. This was it. I straightened my shoulders and held my head high, just the way Ben

Jones had taught me in all his torturous etiquette classes. Then I closed my eyes and listened for the Voice of God.

Gently, I felt a stirring in my spirit when I heard Him whisper, ***I am with you.***

I turned back to the king who sat patiently waiting. "Shakespeare is dead."

The crowd gasped and the king's eyes opened wide. "How? When did this happen? And how can we know you are telling the truth and aren't the murderer yourself!?" The king raised his voice a bit, but it didn't bother me.

I stepped forward and said, "I know, because I am Shakespeare."

There wasn't a single gasp. There was laughter. I felt my ears burning from embarrassment, and my heart began to beat faster, but when the laughing died down, I went into a short explanation.

"I am William Shakespeare. The dramatist of all your favorite plays. I started writing plays as a way out. As a woman, I knew no one would believe me when I told them I had the Gift. So, I wrote a letter to the scribal house under my real name. They immediately accepted me because they wanted to keep my gender a secret."

"You dare blaspheme God? Seize this witch at once!" the king ordered.

Men dressed in heavy armor began to surround us. Guests moved quickly out of the way, making room for the incoming soldiers.

"Wait!"

The men came to a jarring stop. From within my sleeve, I pulled out my wax stamper.

"I have sealed every letter, and every play with this wax stamper. It has my initial on it. You see, I was chosen by God to be a Scribe. He named me before I was even born. My name means 'Man of wisdom, truth and integrity,' in Latin, Hebrew, and Greek."

The room's temperament shifted, like some of them were starting to believe me. I glanced around, catching glimpses of the curious faces. Most of the onlooking men and women seemed interested in what I had to say, or at the very least, interested in the drama of it all. Most of them wore question marks on their faces, some held angry exclamation points, others wore a comma, waiting for me to continue. The king wore all three. He burned with anger that I would blaspheme God, but he was confused because something had begun to make sense, all while he hoped I would continue. And I did, after I handed the stamper off to one of the soldiers.

"I am a woman with the Gift. I've had it all my life, and I created Shakespeare as a way to get me to where I needed to go, which was right here. I thought I'd never get here. And I kind of lost my way as I came to this point. I started to lose focus on what God gave me the Gift for. But, recently, I remembered it.

"Scribes aren't meant to change the course of history; we aren't meant to change anything. We've been given this knowledge of languages to unite people, not erase them. Our purpose as Scribes is to bring unity by sharing the message of Christ. We are to share His Gospel and continue reminding everyone of His return. And we do that by translating the Word of God. So today, I have come with a gift." I motioned to Black. "I was told the proper way to greet a king, is to bring him a gift worthy of his stature. I believe what I have brought you is far greater than any earthly crown."

I turned to Black as he stepped forward and pulled out the book. Over his shoulder, Ray caught my eyes. They widened as a smile crept onto his nervous face. I extended a hand, and he took it. Together, we turned and walked through the guards and up to the king. His face no longer held an exclamation point, and his question mark was fading. Ray knelt first, then I knelt beside him, offering the leatherbound book to the king.

"My name is Favian Amana Hart, and I am a Scribe. I am here today to offer you this gift on behalf of myself, and my husband, and our household."

The king reached forward and shakily received the book in his own hands.

"God told me what to give you," I explained. "As of

now, I am the only Scribe able to read both Hebrew and Greek. It took me a very long time. Many mistakes forced me to start over again. Nonetheless, I have presented you with something I believe would be suitable for you and for the people, men and women alike. It is the first time this language has been translated as purely and plainly since the Geneva version."

The king silently looked over the book. The crowd watched in awe as he turned it over and read the binding, gasping aloud at the words. Across the front of the black book was a title written in gold, **HOLY BIBLE**. Printed along the spine were the initials, **KJV**, and just beneath the initials were the words, **King James Version**.

ACKNOWLEDGEMENTS

I want to acknowledge Jesus Christ as my Lord and Savior and the coming Messiah. I also want to acknowledge my family; you guys are the best! As well as my late grandmother, Bernice Lee, I love you.

The Rebel Christian Publishing

We are an independent Christian publishing company focused on fantasy, science fiction, and YA reads. Visit therebelchristian.com to check out our other books!

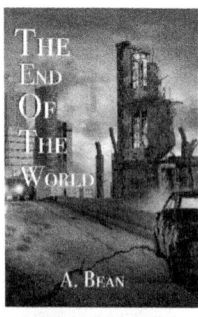

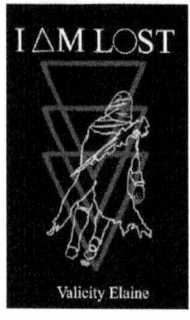

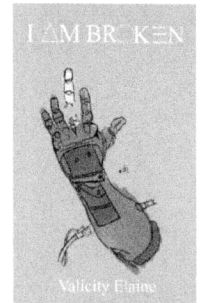

Original Author's Notes

Chapter One
This chapter was actually much longer in the first edit! It was a little tough to condense everything, but I think we got it all in! I'm excited for Amana's trip, I hope you are, too.

Chapter Two
The last scene was tough for me to write. I love Ma, so I hated depicting her as this terrible person. Maybe there is more to her story? We'll see soon!

Chapter Three
I was very excited for this chapter! This is where we learn more about Amana and her inspiration. What role does her faith play in this story? I believe it makes her stronger.

Chapter Four
What do you think of Ma's confession and the story behind Amana's name? I hope we'll see more of "Favian" in the future!

Chapter Five

So Favian is a Scribe but not Amana?? I wonder how this will play out!

Chapter Six

This chapter was one of the easiest to write. I wanted to speed things up a bit and bring in the fun twist of the story, Shakespeare. Not only that, I wanted a turning point in the story, but not just a leap through time, where we would miss all of Amana's growth. I wanted us to grow with Amana while skipping what we needed. I hope you enjoy this little time jump!

Chapter Seven

Chapter seven really gets in the head and heart of Amana. I definitely missed Ray, so I brought him back. I think Ray plays such a vital role in Amana's life, outside of a love interest. He really rounds her out and brings in a "normal" point of view. Besides Ray and Amana, we are now seeing the rise of Shakespeare. I love the way this rise in her career plays background a bit in this chapter.

Chapter Eight

I loved her reasoning for writing "Romeo and Juliet"! It was a simple explanation, but I think that if Shakespeare had truly been a woman, that may have been a reason for writing that play. My favorite part of this chapter was the conversation between Amana and the son of the tailor. She was very elegant, in my opinion, and very strong, which we don't see often from Amana. Ben and Marlowe returning was even a bit frightening for me!

Chapter Nine

Losing Ben was a loss I wasn't sure how to move forward with. I wrestled a bit with losing Ben because of his stagnant character, and the bridging he did for us between Amana and the Scribal world. It was between Ray and Ben, which one would die. Ultimately, Ben dies, however, Ray getting shot was not part of the plan! It kind of just happened, but I think it worked out really well.

Chapter Ten

Finally, we see Jesus! This was my favorite chapter to write so far. I loved bringing Jesus in and having us actually see Jesus. It's almost like He walks right into the room with us! Jesus was actually introduced because I didn't want Ray to be in recovery for a long time. So I brought in the miracle worker Himself, to step past time and perform a miracle. [See **Matthew 16:15-17** for scripture reference]

Chapter Eleven

This chapter was the hardest to write. I didn't enjoy it as much as the others I have written. However, the purpose of this chapter is important, and I felt it was needed.

Chapter Twelve

This chapter was long, however, it was my favorite. Telling the story of our hero, Ben Jones, was actually something I wrote a while ago. Seeing his final words come to life was satisfying and I hope they told a story of a coward who redeemed himself.

Chapter Thirteen

Macbeth, one of my favorite plays of Shakespeare! I didn't want to dive too heavily into this play, but I wanted it to be impactful to readers when they saw Marlowe unfold to become Amana's inspiration for Macbeth.

Chapter Fourteen

Another note from Ben appears in this chapter. I didn't want us to forget Ben, as his role in Amana's life will always be vital to her growth. I also wanted to reach back to some of the concepts introduced earlier in the story (ie women weren't allowed to read the New Testament) to bring everything together as Amana really discovers herself.

Chapter Fifteen

The end of this chapter was amazing to me. I wanted to end this story at a point where readers can imagine what may have taken place. Was Amana accepted for who she was as Shakespeare? Or did they throw her in prison and that's why we've never heard of her before? I've left that up to you! Nonetheless, I want to thank you for following along. I hope you all enjoyed Amana's journey through history.

Printed in Great Britain
by Amazon